A Thou
Hannah. For The First Time
Since Their Marriage Had Been
Arranged, She And Prince Phillip—
No, *King* Phillip—Were Alone.

Totally alone.

In the past, whenever they met, there had always been a chaperone present. But right here, right now, there was no one to stop them from… whatever.

Suddenly she felt ultra-aware of his presence. The clean, crisp scent of his aftershave. The weight of his gaze as he studied her. He was just so…*there*.

And so close.

With little more than a lift of her hand, she could touch him, brush her fingertip across his cheek.

"If you keep chewing your lips that way, there'll be nothing left for me," he teased, and something playfully wicked flashed behind his eyes.

Dear Reader,

Welcome to the first book in my ROYAL SEDUCTIONS series. This is my first series for Desire and I couldn't be more excited, nor could I have picked a more interesting family to write about than the Royals of Morgan Isle, a small island country located in the Irish Sea between England, Scotland, Ireland and Wales.

Phillip is everything you would expect from a king. Gorgeous, wealthy and powerful. And let's not forget *stubborn*. This arranged marriage is nothing to him but that. An arrangement. But Hannah Renault, his bride-to-be, wants the real thing, and she'll stop at nothing to chip away the ice covering his frozen heart.

I hope you enjoy their story!

And you don't have to wait even a month for the next book in this series. Phillip's illegitimate brother, Prince Ethan, has his own story out this month as well. Don't miss *The Illegitimate Prince's Baby* on sale in Silhouette Desire *now!*

Best,

Michelle

THE KING'S
CONVENIENT
BRIDE

MICHELLE CELMER

Published by Silhouette Books
America's Publisher of Contemporary Romance

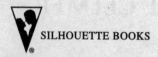

SILHOUETTE BOOKS

ISBN-13: 978-0-373-76876-9
ISBN-10:   0-373-76876-1

THE KING'S CONVENIENT BRIDE

Copyright © 2008 by Michelle Celmer

Visit Silhouette Books at www.eHarlequin.com

Printed in U.S.A.

Books by Michelle Celmer

Silhouette Desire

The Millionaire's Pregnant Mistress #1739
The Secretary's Secret #1774
Best Man's Conquest #1799
The King's Convenient Bride #1876
The Illegitimate Prince's Baby #1877

Silhouette Intimate Moments

Running on Empty #1342
Out of Sight #1398

Silhouette Special Edition

Accidentally Expecting #1847

*Royal Seductions

MICHELLE CELMER

Bestselling author Michelle Celmer lives in southeastern Michigan with her husband, their three children, two dogs and two cats. When she's not writing or busy being a mom, you can find her in the garden or curled up with a romance novel. And if you twist her arm real hard you can usually persuade her into a day of power shopping.

Michelle loves to hear from readers. Visit her Web site at: www.michellecelmer.com, or write her at P.O. Box 300, Clawson, MI 48017.

To my mom, Karen,
who is hands down my most devoted fan.

One

Though she had been preparing for this day for eight years, as the limo pulled up to the palace steps and Hannah Renault caught her first glimpse of the prince—make that the *king*—waiting to welcome her, she trembled in her ecru Gucci pumps.

Wearing his royal dress uniform, King Phillip Lindall Augustus Mead stood at the top of the stairs flanked by what had to be the entire palace staff. A collection of medals and commendations on his jacket glittered in the sun and a gilded sword hung at his hip.

Outside the gates, residents of Morgan Isle crowded to get their first glimpse of their soon-to-be queen.

Aka: *Her.*

The limo stopped at the base of a gold-rimmed red carpet. The door swung open and a gloved hand appeared to help her out.

She smoothed the skirt of her dark blue linen suit. *This is it,* she told herself. This is the day you've been dreaming of. The time to make a good impression on your husband-to-be and, from the looks of it, half the country. So, whatever you do, as you're climbing those stairs, *don't trip.*

With all the grace and dignity a woman could manage while climbing out of a vehicle, her heart fluttering madly in her chest, Hannah stepped into the balmy sunshine. Beyond the gates a cheer broke out among the onlookers.

Warring with the sudden, intense urge to turn around and dive back into the limo, she took a deep breath, straightened her spine and lifted her chin high. As per the instructions she received from the royal social secretary, she stood her ground and waited for the king's formal greeting. She held her breath as he descended the steps and a deafening hush fell over the crowd, as though they were holding their breath with her. *Don't be nervous,* she told herself, but nervous didn't even come close to what she was actually feeling. She bordered more along the lines of *terrified.*

Just breathe, Hannah. In and out. You can do this.

It had been two long years since she had seen her fiancé face-to-face, and he was more handsome, more heart-stoppingly beautiful than she remembered.

As instructed, the instant the king's foot hit the bottom step, Hannah stepped forward and dipped into a routinely practiced curtsy. With a bow of her head, and in a wobbly voice, she said, "Your Highness."

"My lady," he returned in a deep, rich voice, with proper British inflection, then offered his hand. A small burst of energy arced between their fingers an instant before they actually touched. When she met his eyes, something warm and inviting swam in their smoky-gray depths. Taking her hand gently in his own, he bent at the waist and brushed his lips across her skin. "Welcome home."

Her stomach bottomed out and her legs went weak while thunderous applause rattled her eardrums.

You must appear regal and confident, but never *cold,* she had been told a million times from her royal-appointed etiquette coach.

But under the circumstances, it was all she could do to stay upright and conscious.

This was really happening. In two weeks she would marry this handsome, powerful man. In two weeks, she would be a *queen.*

Shaking with excitement and fear, from her toes all the way to the ends of her hair, she allowed him to lead her up the steps, chanting to herself: *please don't trip, please don't trip*.

Picking up on her abject terror, and in a serious break of royal tradition, he slipped his arm around her waist and drew her close to his side. Then he dipped his head and said in a low whisper, so only she could hear, "Relax. The worst is over."

She was so grateful she nearly dissolved into tears right there on the steps. He felt so solid and sturdy and he radiated self-assurance. If there were only a way she could absorb a bit of that confidence for herself.

They reached the top step, where they would stop and she would formally greet the staff and country. But in another breech of ceremony, the king swept past the receiving lines and led her directly to the enormous, gilded double doors that, seemingly on their own, swung open to welcome her inside.

He led her through the cavernous foyer. Two royal attendants were close behind them, the soles of their shoes clicking against the polished marble floor. He stopped in front of a pair of ceiling-high, carved mahogany doors.

"Give us a minute," he told the two attendants, which Hannah took to mean they were not to be disturbed. Then he ushered her inside and closed the door behind them.

She found herself surrounded on three sides by bookshelves that climbed high to kiss the outer rim of an ornately painted cathedral ceiling. She'd never seen so many books in one room. Not even in the university library back home. Furniture upholstered in a rich, deep red leather formed a sitting area in the center of the room. He led her to a chair and ordered, "Sit."

Her legs were so shaky it was that or fall over, so she sat, and took what was probably her first full breath since the limo pulled up to the wrought iron gates.

"Shall I get the smelling salts?" he asked.

For an instant, she thought he might be angry, and she couldn't really blame him, considering how seriously she had blown it, but, when she looked up, he wore the shadow of an amused grin.

She shook her head. "I think I'm okay now."

He crossed the room to the wet bar, chose a decanter and poured a splash of amber liquid into a glass. She thought it was for him, but then he carried it over and pressed it into her hand. "Sip. *Slowly.*"

She sipped and it burned a path of liquid fire down her throat all the way to her belly, temporarily stealing the air from her lungs. When she could breath again, she wheezed, "I'm sorry."

He crouched down beside her chair, leaning on the arm. "For what?"

"I really blew it out there."

"How's that?"

"I was supposed to greet the staff."

He shrugged. "So, you'll greet them later."

"And we were supposed to turn and wave to the people outside the gates."

Again with the shrug. "What they don't know won't hurt them."

She worried her lower lip with her teeth. "But I don't want people to think I'm a snob."

"Are you?"

His question threw her. "Well…no. Of course not. But—"

"Then don't worry about it."

"Isn't it kind of important that the people of the country like me?"

"They will," he assured her, as if he had no doubt.

"What about the press?" Reporters in the States were sometimes brutal, but she'd been warned the media in Europe could be downright vicious.

Phillip didn't look the least bit concerned. "See this?" he asked, indicating his left jacket pocket. "This is where I keep the press. In other words, you have nothing to worry about."

Oh, well, that was good to know. It seemed as

though he had all his bases covered. And why wouldn't he? He was the richest, most powerful man in the country.

She took another sip of her drink, felt the knots in her belly begin to unravel. "My coach insisted I was prepared for this. You can bet she's going to hear from me."

"You did fine. You will grow accustomed to it."

She sure hoped so.

A moment of awkward silence followed and she racked her brain for something to say. Since turning sixteen, everything she had done, all that she had learned, had been in preparation for this day. Now that she was finally here, she was at a total loss.

It wasn't helping that, technically, she was supposed to be marrying a prince. She should have had an indeterminate number of years as a princess, time to adjust to the lifestyle. But the queen's death had unexpectedly moved plans forward.

Phillip, now as king, needed a queen to stand by his side. Even more important, he needed an heir. So, instead of a courtship, in which they would have six months to get to know one another before they took the plunge, they had two very short weeks before they said their *I do's.*

Two weeks.

She downed the contents of her glass, the sting of

the alcohol sucking the air from her lungs and making her eyes well up.

His expression somewhere between amusement and curiosity, he took the glass from her and set it on a nearby table. "Feeling better?"

She nodded, but it was pretty obvious from the crooked, wry smile he wore that he didn't believe her. And it dawned on her, as she glanced around the quiet, empty room, that for the first time since this marriage had been arranged, she and Phillip were alone.

Totally alone.

In the past, to keep things proper and by the book, on the rare occasions they visited each other, there had always been a chaperone present. Though Hannah's experience with the queen had been limited to a few obligatory and brief meetings, she'd heard the rumors. She'd heard that the queen was cold, heartless and ruthlessly demanding.

It was her way or the highway.

But the queen was gone now, and right here, in this empty room, there was no one to stop them from…whatever.

Suddenly she felt ultra aware of his presence. The clean, crisp scent of his aftershave. The weight of his gaze as he studied her. He was just so…*there*.

And so close.

It would take little more than a fraction of movement and she could touch his sleeve. With a lift of her hand she could brush her fingertip across his smooth cheek. And the idea of touching him made her legs feel all wobbly again.

"If you keep chewing your lip that way, there'll be nothing left for me," he teased, and something playfully wicked flashed behind his eyes.

Oh, boy.

In all of the years she'd studied in preparation for this marriage, she had learned about things like etiquette and social graces, bloodlines and royal custom, but no one ever taught her about this kind of stuff. Sure, it had been drilled in her head that she would be expected to produce at least one heir, preferably more, but all advice stopped *outside* the bedroom door.

And to say she was a novice was a gross understatement.

Though her high school girlfriends and college sorority sisters often questioned her sanity, she had made the decision a long time ago, even before the arranged marriage, that she would save herself for her husband on their wedding night.

She and Phillip had never kissed. Never so much as held hands. Not that she hadn't wanted to. But it wouldn't have been *proper.* Right now, here in this room, there wasn't a single thing to stop them.

The idea made her both excited and terrified at the same time. The truth of the matter was, she barely knew him, and that had never been more evident to her than at this very moment.

He leaned forward a fraction and she just about jumped out of her skin. With an amused grin, he asked, "Do I make you nervous, Hannah?"

She took a deep breath, fighting the urge to gnaw her lip. "You're a king. It is a tad intimidating."

"I'm just a man."

Yeah, kind of like The Beatles were *just* a rock-and-roll band or the Mona Lisa is *just* a painting.

"I've been anticipating this day for a really long time," she said, hoping her voice didn't sound as wobbly to his ears as it did to her own.

"Well then, I'll do my best not to disappoint you." His eyes searched her face and she wondered what he was looking for. What did he see when he looked at her? Did he know deep in his heart, just as she did, that they were perfectly suited? Was he as excited about the future as she was?

Though her parents insisted she wait until she was eighteen before making the decision to marry Phillip, from the day she met him, she knew that she would someday be his wife. Had he felt it, too?

With all of her dedication and careful planning, how could their life together not be storybook perfect?

"You are beautiful." He lifted one hand to her face, brushed the backs of his fingers across the curve of her jaw. Her skin warmed and tingled and a funny tickle rippled through her belly. "Does it strike you odd that we'll be married in two weeks, and yet I've never even kissed you?"

"It would have been difficult with the chaperone watching our every move. Of course, that was the point of the chaperone, I guess."

He leaned in the tiniest bit and her heart went berserk. "There's no chaperone here."

"Well," she said, with a confidence she'd dredged up from God only knew where. "I guess now is your big chance."

A grin curled his mouth. He slipped his fingers across her cheek, cupped her face with one large but gentle hand, and goose bumps broke out across her skin. "I guess it is."

Two

Maybe it wasn't proper, but as he leaned in she felt herself tipping forward to meet him halfway. Since she was sixteen years old, she had imagined kissing him, so sue her if she was more than a little enthusiastic.

Her eyes slipped closed and she felt the whisper of his breath, then his lips brushed hers...

Across the room the doors flew open and Hannah was so startled, she shot to her feet.

Phillip sighed and sat back on his heels. Leave it to his sister, Sophie, to kill a moment.

Sophie merely smiled.

He rose to his feet to stand beside his fiancée. She was red-faced with embarrassment, or maybe arousal. Or perhaps a bit of both. "Hannah, you remember my sister, Princess Sophie?"

"Of course," Hannah said, executing a flawless curtsy. "It's so nice to see you again, Your Highness."

"As I'm sure my brother will tell you, I don't care much for titles." She offered Hannah her hand for a firm, very unroyal shake. "From now on, it's just plain old Sophie, okay?"

Hannah nodded, her lip clamped between her teeth. A habit he found rather charming. If it weren't for his sister and her most inconvenient timing, he might be the one chewing that plump, tender flesh.

"I wanted to let you know that the receiving line has been moved to the foyer," Sophie told him. And added with a wry grin, "If you're *ready,* of course."

He turned to his bride-to-be. "Hannah?"

"Is there a powder room I could use first? I have the feeling I gnawed off the last of my lipstick."

"Of course." He gestured to the door. "Right through there."

"I'll try to hurry."

"Take all the time you need."

He watched her cross the room, noting that in

spite of her apprehension, she carried herself with the utmost grace and dignity. It was hard to believe it had been two years since their last meeting. And the fault was entirely his own. Since his father's death he had been too busy to give his impending marriage much attention. There wasn't even supposed to be a marriage for at least another year. Not that he would be any less opposed to the idea then, as he was now.

If it were up to him, he would *never* tie the knot. The idea of being chained to a single woman for the rest of his life sounded so…claustrophobic. But he had a duty to his country. One that he did not take lightly.

And unlike his father, from whom Phillip had inherited his restless nature, he intended to be faithful to his wife.

"You certainly don't waste any time," his sister said. "Although, in the future, you might want to lock the door."

He shot her a warning look.

"It's a good thing the powder room has only one exit," she said. "Or I fear your betrothed might just make a run for it."

He wouldn't even justify that with a response. "Surely you have something better to do."

Sophie grinned. There was nothing she loved more than ruffling his feathers. From the time she was old enough to form words, she had been the con-summate, bratty younger sister.

"Your intended is quite lovely," she said.

"Yes, quite," he agreed. Everything a king could want or expect in a wife.

Though at first the idea of an arranged marriage had been archaic even to him, at the insistence of his mother—who had rejected the concept of the word *no*, unless, of course, she was the one speaking it—he had flown to the States to meet the young woman.

It had been clear to him immediately that at the age of sixteen Hannah already possessed great potential. Despite the eight-year age difference, he found her undeniably attractive. And he could see that the feeling was mutual. And even better, were he to acquiesce, it would keep his parents off his back. At his own request, future meetings were arranged, and plans for a courtship were set in motion.

By eighteen she had blossomed into a woman of exceptional beauty and poise, and their feelings had matured from ones of sexual curiosity to intense physical attraction.

She was everything a king could want in a mate, and right now her innocence, her eagerness to please, appealed to him. Sadly, he was easily bored and quite sure that the novelty would soon wear off.

"Do you think she has the slightest clue what she's getting herself into?" Sophie asked.

"The slightest." There was only so much she could learn from a book or a tutor. The rest would come through experience.

"While I have you here, I was hoping to have a word with you."

He felt an argument coming on. "If this is about what I think it's about—"

"He's our *brother.* You could at least hear him out."

"Half brother," he said firmly. A product of their father's infidelity. "I owe him nothing."

"What he is proposing would ensure the stability of our empire for *generations.*"

"And his own, no doubt."

She looked at him as though he were loony. "You say that like it's a *bad* thing."

"I don't trust him."

"If it's the crown that concerns you, he wants no part of it."

Not unlike Sophie, he thought, who had spent the better part of her twenty-five years expressing her dislike of the monarchy's rules. But in the case of their half brother, Ethan Rafferty, their father's blood ran through his veins. As a result, he did have a claim to the crown. If something were to happen to Phillip, he would be next in line.

For Phillip, that was unacceptable.

"I won't discuss this," Phillip told her. "Period."

Her cheeks flushed with frustration. "Bloody hell, you're stubborn!"

She was one to talk. "That distinction, dear Sophie, is not limited to me."

The door to the powder room opened, and Hannah emerged. Grateful for the interruption, he crossed the room to meet her. "Feeling better?"

Hannah nodded. "I think I'm ready to do this. And I'm sorry again for getting so freaked out."

"Were you?" Sophie asked from behind him. "I'm quite sure no one noticed."

Hannah cracked an appreciative smile. The first one he had seen since she arrived.

He offered his arm to her. "Shall I escort you?"

She looked from his arm to the door, then took a deep breath. "I appreciate the offer, but I think that after what happened outside, it's important that I stand on my own two feet."

"As you wish." He opened the door for her and watched, feeling an unexpected surge of pride as she swept out into the foyer.

Sophie stepped up beside him and, in a quiet voice, said, "Impressive."

"Indeed."

"You think she's ready for this?"

He nodded, and said with genuine honesty, "I do."

"I agree," she said. "The real question, Your Highness, is are *you* ready for *her?*"

This day turned out to be, by far, the most demanding, frightening and exciting in Hannah's life. After the receiving line, which in itself took the better part of an hour, they attended a luncheon in her honor. Following a meal she had been too self-conscious to do more than pick at, she and the king mingled with dozens of state officials and their spouses. So many, in fact, that remembering all of their names would take nothing short of a miracle.

After lunch there was a photo shoot in the garden, followed by a short press conference in which she and the king were bombarded by the reporters with questions of her background and education, how she felt about becoming queen, their upcoming nuptials and the plans for the gala to celebrate the country's 500th anniversary.

To stand beside the king, to feel the air of confidence and supremacy all but spilling from his pores, was as fascinating as it was intimidating. He was the most powerful man in the country and he embraced the designation. And for what wasn't the first time that day, she couldn't help but wonder if she'd gotten in way over her head. Years of training and preparation and still she felt overwhelmed. She knew though, had her father been there, he would have been so proud of her, and that was all that mattered.

She endured another exhausting evening meal shared with a new blur of names and faces she barely had a hope of remembering, although there was one woman she recognized from earlier in the day. And only because of the way she watched Hannah so intently. She was dark and very beautiful, close to Hannah's age, if not a year or two older. She had the kind of voluptuous figure that turned men's heads. Hannah considered going to talk to her, but that would require leaving Phillip's side, and she wasn't ready to do that yet. But every time Hannah looked her way, the woman was watching. Shamelessly and blatantly. But just as Hannah began to feel uncomfortable, the woman vanished. She craned her neck, checking every corner of the room, but didn't see her.

That was odd. And she couldn't shake the feeling she had imagined her.

After another hour of small talk and chatter, the king finally bid the guests good-night and offered to escort Hannah to her suite.

She was so exhausted, the thought of collapsing into bed made her want to weep with relief.

Offering his arm, Phillip led her to the private residence at the north end of the palace. Though it may have been used only by the family and limited staff, it was no less luxurious than the common areas. More modern, and not nearly so formal, but dripping in extravagance and style. Her parents' estate in Seattle was by no means small, but wealth of this magnitude was foreign to her.

It would take some getting used to.

The instant they were inside with the door closed, he unfastened the button at the collar of his jacket and, just like that, transformed back into the less intimidating version of himself—the compassionate man who had whisked her up the palace steps and inside to the sanctuary of the library.

"You did well today," he told her.

"To be honest, it's all a bit of a blur." And all she could comprehend at the present moment was the pain in her feet. The desperate need to kick out of the pumps the salesgirl had assured her would spare her any discomfort. *Like walking on a cloud, my foot.*

"Would it be possible to get a photo and bio of the government officials?" she asked.

He regarded her curiously. "What for?"

"So I can learn their names. I met so many people tonight, I have no hope of remembering them all and I don't want to appear rude. That should include information of their spouses and families as well. I'm assuming you can do that."

The king looked surprised and impressed. "Of course. You'll have it first thing tomorrow."

They stopped outside what she assumed was her suite. "I have to apologize for the temporary accommodations," he said. "This suite is somewhat small."

She didn't care about the size. So long as it had a tub to soak in and a bed to melt into, he wasn't going to hear her complaining. "I'm sure it will be fine."

He opened the door. "You'll stay here while the permanent suite is being renovated. In fact, I believe you have an appointment with the decorator tomorrow afternoon."

She didn't want to think any further ahead than a hot bubble bath, but as he led her inside, she found herself facing three more new faces. Two were dressed in formal black-and-white maid's uniforms and the other in a modest, navy-blue pinstripe business suit.

"Hannah, I'd like to introduce you to your staff. Miss Cross and Miss Swan, your personal maids, and your personal assistant, Miss Pryce."

All three curtsied and said in unison, "My lady."

She smiled and said, "It's a pleasure to meet you."

Miss Pryce stepped forward, a leather-bound folder tucked under one arm. "I have your schedule, my lady, and your agenda for tomorrow."

"My fiancée is quite exhausted," Phillip said. "I think this can wait until morning."

She nodded and retreated a step. "My apologies, sir."

With little more than a flick of his wrist and tilt of his head, he dismissed her staff. "Your suite includes a sitting room, sleeping chamber and office."

"And a bathroom, I hope."

He smiled. "Of course. With all the amenities you could possibly need. In your office you'll see that you've been supplied with all the computer equipment you asked for."

"Thanks." She turned in a circle, taking in the decor. The room was decorated in neutral shades of brown and beige and the furniture looked comfortable and inviting. It was more than large enough to suit her. Larger even than her residence on her parents' estate. She wasn't sure why they would go through the trouble of decorating a suite especially for her since, after the wedding, she would be sharing a suite with her husband.

Or maybe they would be moving into the new suite together. In which case it was nice of him to let her do the decorating. To extend that sort of trust to a woman he barely knew. "It's lovely, and more than adequate."

"Excellent." He removed his jacket and tossed it over the arm of a chair. Underneath he wore a plain,

white long-sleeved knit shirt, similar to a mock tur-
tleneck. It clung to the contours of his chest and
arms, accentuating what appeared to be toned,
defined muscle underneath. Even without the bulk of
his jacket, the expansive width of his shoulders was
impressive to say the least.

She wondered how it would feel to put her hands
on him. How would his arms feel around her?

The thought of him touching her, and their almost-
kiss in the library, had her blushing from her toes to
the ends of her hair.

Once again they were alone together. Just the two
of them, but this time in her suite. Mere steps away
from the bedroom. And Hannah seriously doubted
that Princess Sophie, who she had seen sneaking off
with one of the guests shortly after dinner, would be
around to interrupt them this time.

Is that why he'd sent the staff away? Did he
have…*plans* for them?

He walked across the room to a cabinet that held
a dozen or so decanters of alcohol, chose one and
poured them each a drink. He turned to her, looking
surprised to see that she was still rooted firmly to the
same spot.

"It's been a long day," he said, walking toward her.
"Sit down. Relax."

Her feet were throbbing, but the idea of taking off

her shoes while he was in the room made her feel
so...*vulnerable.* "You're staying?"

"Would you prefer I leave?"

"No, of course not. I just... Is this okay?"

He set both drinks on the table beside the couch.
"Is what okay?"

"You being in my suite. You know...before the
wedding."

He shrugged. "Why wouldn't it be?"

"It's not against the rules?"

"Is there a reason it should be?"

Why did she get the feeling he was making this
up as he went along? "Next you'll be telling me it's
all right for you to tuck me into bed."

His mouth tipped up in a feral smile. "If that's
what you wish."

He was teasing her again, and she was a little
stunned to realize that she was teasing him right
back. It was...empowering. And a little scary.

"As you pointed out earlier, I'm a king. I make the
rules." He gestured to the couch. "Join me?"

Her feet were killing her, and God knows it would
feel absolutely wonderful to sit down. Maybe just for
a little while.

She took a step forward, then hesitated.

"Don't worry. I don't bite." A grin split his face.
"Unless, of course, you would *like* me to."

She bit her lip.

"You can trust me," he assured her.

Maybe that wasn't the problem. Maybe it wasn't Phillip's behavior that she questioned.

Maybe it was herself she didn't trust.

Three

Phillip sighed.

He had things to do tonight. A long-awaited task to accomplish, but she wasn't making this easy. Of course, he probably wasn't helping matters. But he did so very much enjoy teasing her. "I promise to be on my best behavior."

She surprised him again by folding her arms across her chest and saying, "With no frame of reference, how can I begin to know what your best behavior is?"

He liked Hannah, and was saddened by the thought that it wouldn't last. That someday soon he would grow bored with her. But he might as well enjoy it while it lasted. "How about I promise to keep my hands to myself? All right?"

She considered that, and he wasn't sure if she looked relieved or disappointed. Finally, she nodded. "All right."

She walked to the couch and sat primly on the edge of the cushion—knees pressed firmly together and tipped to one side—smoothing the creases from her skirt and jacket. He sat beside her, far enough away that it would be considered proper by anyone's standards.

"Feel free to remove the torture devices from your feet," he said, and at her look of confusion, added, "Your shoes. They look uncomfortable."

She glanced down, a pained look on her face, then blatantly lied to him by saying, "They feel fine."

Why did she have to be so…difficult? He wasn't exactly looking forward to what he had to do, but it would go much more smoothly if she would just relax.

He handed her a drink, watched as she took a sip, then he took a healthy swallow of his own. Hopefully the alcohol would loosen her up a bit. Make this less painful for both of them. Not that he thought she would voice an objection once he got started.

He had considered the garden as a more suitable location. More romantic, he supposed, but more than likely someone would have seen. In a life so very public, he felt he deserved a few private moments. Especially for an act as intimate as the one he was about to perform.

Maybe it was like taking off a bandage. The faster he did it, the less it would sting.

He downed the last of his brandy then took Hannah's barely touched glass from her and set them both on the table.

Well, here goes.

With Hannah watching him curiously, he lowered himself to the floor beside the couch on one knee and produced the small velvet box from his pants pocket.

Hannah's eyes went wide and her mouth fell open in surprise before she caught herself and snapped it shut again.

He flipped the box open to reveal the fourteen-carat diamond ring that had been passed down through his family for the past twelve generations. Hannah gasped softly.

Breaking his promise not to touch her, he took her hand in his. "Hannah Renault, would you do me the honor of becoming my wife?"

In a soft, breathy voice, she said, "Of course I will."

He lifted the ring from the satin pillow that was inside the velvet box and slipped it on her ring finger, feeling the sickening sensation of his freedom slithering from his grasp.

He let go of her hand and she stared in wonder at the enormous rock on her finger. When she looked back up at him, a pool of tears welled in her eyes.

Bloody hell, did she have to go and do that? As if this wasn't awkward enough. But for her sake, he did his best to hide his discomfort. Besides, what woman wouldn't get a little misty-eyed to have such a fine piece of jewelry in her possession?

"I've never seen anything so beautiful," she said wistfully.

Or so big, he imagined. If there was one constant with women, it was a love of things that sparkled. "It's been in my family for generations."

"It's amazing."

The moisture building in her eyes hovered precariously at the edge of lids, threatening to spill over at any second. A good reason for him to—as the Americans liked to say—get the hell out of Dodge.

He shifted his weight, preparing to pull himself to his feet, but before he got the chance, she vaulted off the couch, threw her arms around his neck and hugged him.

In all of her preparations for this marriage, not even in the instructions that had been sent to her, breaking down the events of her first day in the palace, had one word been mentioned about a formal proposal. Which, in her mind, could mean only one thing.

He had gotten down on one knee before her not out of duty, but simply because he *wanted* to.

It was the sweetest, most romantic thing anyone had ever done for her. Like her fairy-tale dream coming true. And it was the only logical way to explain how, one minute she was sitting across from him, and the next she was pressed up against him, her arms linked tightly around his neck.

She felt his arms circle her, his large palms settle on and cover the entire width of her hips. He smelled masculine and inviting. And she liked the way their bodies fit together just right. The warm, solid feel of him. He made her feel...safe.

But was she really? His hands were mere inches from parts of her that had never been touched by a man. Parts that shouldn't be touched for at least another two weeks. Then his grip on her tightened almost imperceptibly.

A warm shiver of awareness coursed through her from her head all the way to her toes and she was suddenly hyperconscious of not only his body, but of her own. The slight quickening of her breath. The tingle in her breasts where they crushed the solid wall of muscle in his chest. She could even feel the heat of his skin seeping through the layers of their clothing.

A hot curl of desire started in her belly and spiraled outward in a thrilling rush. Into her arms and legs, her fingers and toes, and some very interesting and wicked places in between.

Every scent and sound and sensation seemed to jumble together, making her feel dizzy and confused. There was an incredible energy building between them. She could feel his breath deepen, his pulse quicken to keep time with her own frantically beating heart.

It was frightening and exciting and arousing all at the same time. And though she knew it was wrong, it felt too good to stop.

Phillip moved his head and Hannah felt the scrape of his beard stubble against her cheek. The warm rush of his breath on her ear. *Pull away,* her conscience warned. *You do not want to do this.*

Oh yes, I do, answered back the part of her that had been looking forward to this for the past eight years.

His lips were so close. So near she could almost taste them. He moved his head, nuzzled her cheek lightly, and everything inside her melted to hot liquid. If she hadn't already been sitting, her legs surely would have buckled out from under her.

Anticipation buzzed between them like an electric, live wire. He turned just a little and she felt his lips…on her cheek, at the corner of her mouth….

His mouth brushed hers and though she was expecting it, longing for it even, it still surprised her. And scared her half to death. It felt too wonderful, and she had come too far, saved herself for too long, to turn back now.

Gathering up the absolute last shred of restraint left in her, she turned and rested her head on his shoulder. "You promised me that you would keep your hands to yourself."

His voice sounded rough when he spoke. "That's not exactly fair, considering you started it."

She couldn't argue with that. She had literally thrown herself at him. The only person to blame here was herself. "You're right. But we have to stop."

"No, we don't." His hands slid from her hips to the indent of her waist. He nuzzled the tender spot just below her ear and she shivered. "You can't tell me that you don't want this as much as I do."

Of course she did, maybe even more, but that wasn't the point. She dropped her arms from around his neck and flattened her palms on his chest. "As you get to know me, you'll find I have this annoying habit of doing things by the book. And we're not married yet."

"No one will know."

"*I'll* know."

He sighed, a long, tired sound tinged with frustration. Then lifted her up, as though she weighed nothing, and deposited her back on the couch.

Since she didn't trust herself and she clearly couldn't rely on him to apply the brakes, from now on there would be no more temptation. That meant no kissing or touching of any kind until after the wedding. "We've waited this long. Two more weeks aren't going to kill us."

He pulled himself to his feet. "Speak for yourself."

She diverted her gaze, finding that it both embarrassed her and gave her a depraved thrill to know that touching her had aroused him. "Are you angry with me?"

The hard lines of his face softened. "Of course not. If more people honored their values the way you do, the world would be a much better place."

Of all the things he could have possibly said to her, that had to have been the sweetest. And he said it so honestly, as though he really meant it. Maybe he wasn't so tough as he liked people to think.

"I should go," he said. "You've had a long day."

"I am exhausted," she admitted. With the time change and the long trip, she had been up for more than twenty-four hours straight.

"There's a directory by the phone if you should need anything." He grabbed his jacket from the chair and walked to the door.

She followed, several steps behind. "Thank you."

He stopped, hand on the doorknob, and turned to her. "For what?"

She shrugged, suddenly feeling embarrassed. She was twenty-four years old and still so terribly naive about certain things. But anxious to learn. "I don't know. *Everything,* I guess."

"You're welcome." He pulled the door open, then hesitated. "By the way, where do you keep your lipstick?"

"Lipstick?"

"You carried no handbag, yet you've freshened your lipstick numerous times throughout the course of the day. I was just wondering where you were hiding it."

It was funny that he had even noticed. Although, she had the sneaking suspicion there wasn't much that the king missed.

She smiled. "A proper lady, Your Highness, never tells."

"I had a feeling you would say that." With a shake of his head, he stepped into the hall, then turned back one last time. "I should warn you, *my lady,* that I am used to getting what I want when I want it. Though we may not officially consummate this relationship until after the wedding." His mouth curled into a hungry, feral smile. "I can't promise that in the meantime there won't be a bit of fooling around."

At first she thought he was only teasing her again, but she could see, by the look in his eyes, that he was dead serious.

She opened her mouth to respond, but nothing came out. What could she possibly say? It occurred to her, not for the first time that day, that she was *way* out of her league.

He flashed her the smile of a man who knew he had just hit his mark. "Good night, Hannah. Sleep well."

The door snapped shut quietly behind him, and she didn't doubt for an instant that he would make good on his threat.

And damned if she barely slept a wink all night.

Four

Hannah was awake, showered and dressed when Miss Pryce knocked on the door to her suite the next morning at 9:00 a.m. on the dot. Beating down a monster case of jet lag, Hannah opened the door and invited her in.

"Good morning, my lady." She curtsied, quite an impressive feat considering her arms were stacked with file folders and binders. "I have the information you requested."

"My gosh, someone must have been up all night compiling this." She shuddered to think of all the reading she had ahead of her. She would have to call down for a second pot of coffee. But with any luck, the mystery woman from yesterday would be among the pages and Hannah might learn her identity. And maybe have some clue as to why she'd watched Hannah so intently.

"Would you like it in your office?" Miss Pryce asked.

She hated being cooped up in an office. "Why don't you set it down on the table by the sofa."

She did as requested then stood stiffly, clutching the leather binder she'd had with her last night. The dreaded schedule.

"Would you care for a cup of coffee, Miss Pryce?"

"No, thank you."

"I could call down for tea."

She didn't even crack a smile. "I'm fine, thank you."

How about a valium, or shot of whiskey? Hannah thought. She wondered if everyone around here was always this formal. If so, it was going to take some serious getting used to. For them, that is. Hannah's staff at home had always been more like an extension of the family than actual employees.

Being royalty didn't mean she had to be a cold fish.

"Do you have a first name, Miss Pryce?"

She looked confused. "Of course."

"What is it?"

She hesitated for an instant, as though she wasn't quite sure why Hannah would even ask. "Elizabeth."

"May I address you by your first name?"

Miss Pryce looked utterly confused.

Hannah sighed. Something this simple shouldn't be so difficult. "Miss Pryce, I'm not sure how things are done here in the palace, but as my personal secretary, I can only assume we'll be spending quite some time together."

Miss Pryce nodded.

"In that case, it would be nice if I could address you by your first name."

"Of course, my lady. I would be honored."

This *my lady* stuff was going to get old fast. "And I don't suppose there would be any chance you could call me Hannah?"

Miss Pryce lowered her eyes and shook her head. "That wouldn't be proper. I would lose my job."

She would push the issue, but Hannah could see that she was making her uncomfortable. After she and Phillip were married, at least her title would change to a less pretentious, *Ma'am*.

"Before we get started, I was hoping to have a word with my fiancé." Since he left her suite last night, she had been anticipating seeing him again. She had a million questions to ask him. Things about him she was dying to know.

"He's not here."

"Oh. Do you know when he'll be back?"

"Friday, I think."

"Friday?" *Five* days?

"If the weather holds," she added.

"Weather?"

"He and his cousin, Sir Charles, don't care to hunt in the rain."

Hunt? He went *hunting?*

She willed herself to remain calm, to ignore the deep spear of disappointment that lodged in her heart. She'd been here less than twenty-four hours and he'd left to go on a *hunting* trip? That would leave them barely a week to get to know one another before the wedding. Didn't he care about her?

Calm down, Hannah. Of course he did. His actions yesterday proved his affection for her. There had to be a logical reason. A hunting trip to disguise business, maybe? Some secret trip no one could know the truth about?

There was no way he would just *leave* her.

Her distress must have shown, because Miss Pryce looked suddenly alarmed. "If it's an emergency—"

"*No.* No emergency." She forced a smile. The last thing she wanted was for her assistant to know how deeply her feelings had been hurt. "It can wait until he returns." Hannah gestured to the sofa. "Shall we get started?"

Hannah sat, and Elizabeth lowered herself stiffly

beside her. Apparently it was going to take time for her to relax in Hannah's presence. Baby steps.

"So, what's on the schedule for today?"

"You meet with the decorator at eleven o'clock, followed by a luncheon at one with the wives of the heads of state."

"That sounds nice." She would be sure to skim the files Elizabeth brought so she could pluck at least a few of their names from memory. "What next?"

She went on, but Hannah was only half listening. Her mind was still stuck on Phillip's abrupt disappearance. Was it possible that he wasn't hunting at all? That he might be with another woman? And what if it was the mystery woman who wouldn't stop staring at her?

She dismissed the thought almost as quickly as it formed. Now she was being paranoid and silly.

She wasn't so naive as to believe that Phillip had saved himself for her. But he'd had the decency to keep that aspect of his life quite discreet. Which told her that he was a man of integrity. And men of integrity were faithful to their significant others.

Finding suspicion with his every action would only make her life miserable.

She was sure that if he had to leave, it was for a good reason. Though Phillip was her fiancé, and would later be her husband, he was a king first and foremost. A servant to his country. That was a fact she would have to accept.

This brief absence would just make them appreciate each other that much more when he returned.

This is just a hiccup, she assured herself. Everything would work out just the way she'd planned.

Phillip stood on the steps leading to the garden, an unseasonably warm breeze ruffling the collar of his shirt, his attention on his future wife.

She sat on a blanket in the shade of a tree whose leaves had just begun to change, legs folded underneath her, hair tumbling in silky chestnut waves down her back. She wore a simple slip dress the exact shade of amber as the turning leaves.

He stepped down onto the grass and walked toward her, finding himself mesmerized by her beauty, intrigued by the intense desire to be near her. To touch her again. In profile, her features looked finely boned and elegant. Regal and confident, with a hint of softness that he found undeniably appealing.

Fine breeding stock, his mother had assured him when the pairing had been suggested and he had yet to meet Hannah, or even see a photo of her. He recalled thinking at the time that his mother could have been describing a head of cattle, not a future member of the family.

Beside her on the blanket sat a pile of binders, and one lay open across her lap. She was so engrossed in whatever it was she was reading, she didn't hear him approach.

"Good afternoon."

She let out a squeak of surprise and the folder tumbled from her lap onto the ground. When she looked up and saw it was him standing there, she scrambled to her feet, which he noticed were bare.

"I'm sorry," she said and executed a slightly wobbly curtsy. "You startled me."

As she straightened, her hair slipped across her shoulders, thick and shiny, resting in loose spirals atop the swell of her breasts. It all but begged to be touched and his fingers itched to tangle in the silky ribbons. From that day forward he would insist that she never wear it up again.

"If I startled you, perhaps *I* should be the one apologizing," he said.

She clasped her hands in front of her, her lip clamped between her teeth, but behind it he could see the shadow of a smile. "You're back sooner than I expected."

Despite that, he would have anticipated her to be angry with him. Seeing as how he had left so abruptly. Instead, she seemed genuinely happy to see him.

It had been selfish and insensitive of him to leave her alone, but a lesson she needed to learn. It was best she understand that he had no intention of changing his habits simply because he had a wife. This was an arrangement, a business deal of sorts. The sooner she realized and accepted that, the better off they would both be.

Which did little to explain why, as she'd pointed out, he was home three days early.

"I had to cut my trip short," he told her.

"Bad weather?" she asked. And, to his look of confusion, added, "Miss Pryce said you don't like to hunt in bad weather."

The weather on the opposite end of the island where the hunting cabin was located had been much like it was here. Idyllic. Clear skies and temperatures ten degrees above the usual for late September. And though the company had been equally adequate—he looked forward to trips with his cousin, when he could relax and just be Phillip—this time he'd felt restless and bored.

"Stop acting like an ass and go home to your fiancée," Charles had urged after having his head all but snapped off for the umpteenth time in two days.

Indignant at first, Phillip was now glad that he'd listened. Best he enjoy the novelty of this relationship while it lasted.

And just for fun, he planned to test the values to which she clung so firmly.

"If you prefer," he said, "I could go back."

"N-no, of course not, I just…" She noticed his wry grin, and flashed a somewhat shy smile of her own. "You're teasing me."

He nodded.

"I'm glad you're home."

Oddly enough, so was he.

He gestured to the work she'd abandoned on the blanket. "Sorry if I disturbed you."

"Not at all. I had some spare time and thought I would catch up on my reading. And take advantage of the mild weather."

"They're keeping you busy?"

"Swamped. It seems as though I've had more meetings in the past three days than in the last two years. And I've met so many new people, their faces and names all blur together. Every time I get a free minute or two, I try to study the profiles."

"I was thinking, since it is such a beautiful day, that you might like to take a walk around the grounds with me."

"I would love to, but…" She glanced from him, to the palace, then to the delicate gold watch on her left wrist.

"Is there a problem?"

"I have a meeting with the decorator in fifteen minutes, then the wedding coordinator after that."

"Not anymore."

She blinked with confusion. "Pardon?"

"I told Miss Pryce to clear your schedule for the rest of the afternoon."

"You did?"

He nodded. "You're free for the remainder of the day."

"Is that okay?" she asked. But before he could answer, she held up a hand and said, "I know, you're the king. You make the rules."

He smiled and held out his hand, found himself eager to touch her again. "Shall we?"

She hesitated, probably remembering her no-fooling-around-until-after-the-wedding rule. But he had no intention of waiting until their wedding night to take her to his bed.

And he would seduce her so cleverly, she would believe it had been her idea in the first place.

"Something wrong?" he asked.

She shook her head, gazing at his hand as though it were a poisonous creature poised to attack.

"Surely you don't find holding hands with your fiancé inappropriate."

"Not exactly."

"Do I frighten you, then?"

"Not in the way you might think. It's more a matter of trust."

"You don't trust me?"

"I don't trust *me*. Women have desires, too, Your Highness."

Her candor both surprised and impressed him, and told him that, despite her resolve, she was as good as him. He'd yet to find a woman able to resist his charms. He doubted that Hannah would be any different.

She finally slipped her hand in his, and he could swear he felt her shiver.

This was going to be *too* easy.

Five

Though Phillip's leaving had been a blip in her carefully laid plans, the instant his hand slipped around her own, the second his fingers threaded loosely through hers, as far as Hannah was concerned, things were back on track.

Dressed in slacks, a plain white button-down shirt and a caramel cashmere sport coat, he looked casual, but carried himself with an air of supremacy that was almost intoxicating. A woman could feed endlessly off the energy he exuded.

They took a long, leisurely stroll through the gardens and, for the first time since she'd arrived, she felt as though she could finally relax. She had begun to feel as though she were being pulled in ten directions at once. Then Phillip appeared, snapped his fingers and made it all go away. Somehow she knew deep down that, no matter what, he would take care of her.

They walked across the pristinely maintained lawn—she'd seen golf courses that didn't look this good—in the general direction of the woods bordering the estate.

"Did you have a successful trip?" she asked.

"You mean, did I kill anything?" he replied, and she nodded. "Not this time."

"What's in season here this time of year? No, wait, let me guess. You're king, so *you* make the rules. You can kill whatever you want, whenever you want."

He grinned and she felt an honest-to-goodness flutter in her heart. She would call his smile beautiful, had he not been so utterly male.

"I have to follow the laws of the land like everyone else," he said. "Right now we're hunting small game and birds."

"Could I go with you sometime?"

"Hunting?"

She nodded, and he looked genuinely surprised.

"My father and I went every year up until his death." A knot of emotion rose up and clogged her throat, the way it always did when she talked about him. Losing him so unnecessarily had left a laceration on her heart that, a year later, was still raw and bleeding.

Everyone kept telling her that it would get easier, but the truth was, each day it seemed to hurt a little bit more. For her anyway. Her mother, it would seem, had little trouble moving on.

"You were close with your father," Phillip said. A statement more than a question.

She nodded, and he gave her hand a squeeze. It was a simple gesture, but it meant everything to her. "He was my hero."

"It was a car accident?"

"His car was hit by a drunk driver. He was killed instantly. Of course, the other driver walked away with barely a scratch. The worst part was that it wasn't the first time. He had three prior convictions for DUI and was driving on a revoked license."

"The laws here are much tougher on repeat offenders than in the U.S."

"It's tough enough losing someone you love, but for it to be so…senseless. It's just not fair."

"No, it isn't," he agreed.

She realized that recently losing a parent was one thing they had in common. "Reports of your mother's death said she was sick, but they never really specified what she died of."

"She had cancer of the liver."

"It must have been quick."

"She was given six months when she was diagnosed. She only lived three."

"There was nothing they could do?"

He shook his head. "It was too far advanced."

She searched his face for a sign of remorse or loss, but there was none. When he spoke of her, he sounded almost...cold. "Do you miss her?"

"I barely knew her." He glanced over at her. "She was cold, overbearing and heartless."

Her parents certainly hadn't been perfect, but she never once doubted their love for her. "That's sad."

He shrugged, as though it didn't bother him in the least. They stopped at the edge of the woods, near the base of a barely perceptible and frightfully narrow path cut through the trees flanked with thick underbrush. "I'd like to show you something."

"Okay."

"It's untended, so watch your step."

He tugged her along after him, the woods swallowing them up, transporting them instantly into a world that was quiet and serene, and rich with the scent of earth and vegetation. Even the sun couldn't penetrate the dense canopy of leaves overhead.

"I'm going to assume there are no dangerous wild animals out here," she said, ducking under a low-hanging branch.

"I assure you, we're perfectly safe."

She followed him for several hundred feet, and could swear she heard the sound of running water. The deeper they descended, the louder it became. Finally they reached a clearing and bisecting the forest was a quaint, bubbling brook. It was like something out of a storybook.

"It's lovely!" she told him.

"My sister and I used to play here when we were children," he said, releasing her hand so she could investigate. "It was forbidden, which made it all the more appealing. We would sneak away from our nanny and spend hours investigating."

And so would her and Phillip's children.

She made her way to the water's edge, and though it probably wasn't *proper,* she couldn't resist toeing off her sandal and dipping into the chilly water. "You were close? You and Sophie?"

"When we were small. But now Sophie and I are very…different."

"How is that?"

"You'll find that my sister is something of a free spirit."

"She's independent?"

"That's putting it mildly."

She might have been imagining it, but she could swear he sounded sad. Maybe he missed the relationship they'd had. If his mother was as cold as he'd described, maybe they were all the other had.

"I always wanted a brother or sister," she told him.

"And ironically, I always wished I were an only child. Siblings are highly overrated."

Somehow she doubted that. "You have a brother, too."

"Half brother." His response was so full of venom, his eyes so icy, it gave her a cold chill. Maybe this was a subject best left alone for the time being. She was sure that once they got to know each other, he would open up more.

One step at a time, she reminded herself.

She slipped back into her sandal, a sudden chill making her shiver. Goose bumps broke out across her arms and she rubbed to warm them.

"You're cold," he said. He shrugged out of his sport coat and slipped it around her. It was warm and soft and smelled like him.

He arranged it on her shoulders, using both hands to ease her hair from underneath it, his fingers brushing the back of her neck. She shivered again, but this time it had nothing to do with the temperature. At least, not the air. Her inner thermostat on the other hand had begun a steady climb.

It was the way he looked at her, so…thoroughly. As though he wanted to devour her with his eyes.

"I like your hair down," he said, brushing it gently back from her face. "Promise me you'll wear it like this all the time."

"I have so much natural curl that when I wear it down, it tends to look kind of…untamed."

His mouth pulled into one of those sexy, simmering smiles. "I know. I like you that way."

Oh, boy, here we go again.

"It wouldn't be proper."

"*Proper* is also highly overrated. Besides, I make the rules. And I hereby decree that, from this day forward, you are to wear your hair down."

She might have been offended if she thought for a second that he was serious about the royal decree thing. Besides, he was standing so close that the testosterone he was giving off was beginning to short-circuit her brain.

He cupped the side of her face, traced her features with his thumb. Her cheek, her brow, the corner of her mouth. Her internal thermometer shot up another ten degrees and her knees started to feel soft and squishy. She knew it would be best to stop him, but they had connected emotionally today. Physical affection just seemed like the natural next step.

Maybe a bit *too* natural.

His eyes searched her face. "You're beautiful, you know."

She took in a deep breath. "Your Highness, I suspect you're trying to seduce me."

"If I am, it seems to be working." His thumb brushed her cheek. "You're blushing."

She didn't have a snappy comeback for that one. And, oh, how she wanted to touch him. To put her hands on his chest and feel his heart beating, feel the warmth of his skin through his shirt. She wanted to run her fingers through his hair, across his face, feel the faint shadow of stubble on his cheeks.

He brushed his fingers across her cheek. "Your skin feels warm here."

Probably because her blood was hovering just below the boiling point.

He stroked lower, down her chin and throat, his eyes following the path of his hand. Then lower still, just above the swell of her breasts. It was a move so intimate and sexually charged, and *wonderful,* that she went weak all over. With desire and fear and curiosity.

He lifted his eyes to hers. "And here."

"Phillip—"

"I know, I'm breaking the no-touching rule." He caressed the uppermost swell of her breasts with the tips of his fingers and her knees nearly buckled with the new, erotic sensation. "But as king, I make my own rules." He leaned in closer, until his mouth was only inches from hers. "And nothing is going to stop me from kissing you."

Well then, there wasn't much point in telling him no, was there? Besides, what harm could one kiss do? A *real* kiss this time. How far could it go, out here in the woods?

"Just one kiss," she told him, as though his demand even required a response.

He cupped her cheek and mini explosions of sensation detonated under her skin.

She was getting that weak, dizzy feeling again. "Then we stop."

His other hand slipped through her hair to cradle the back of her head. He lowered his head and she lifted hers to meet him, her eyes slipping closed. Then their lips touched, barely more than a brush, and time seemed to stand still. It was just her lips and his lips, their breath mingling.

It was unbelievably wonderful. So sweet and gentle, as though she were a delicate piece of china he thought he might break. And while her head was telling her it was time to pull away, time to stop, her heart was telling her just a little longer. Because sweet and gentle wasn't enough for her this time. She wanted more.

Which was why, when Phillip deepened the kiss, when she felt his tongue tease the seam of her lips, she didn't do or say a thing to stop him. And when she gave in, opened up to him, the kiss went from sweet to simmering in the span of a heartbeat.

He tunneled his fingers through her hair, drew her against the length of his long, solid frame. She couldn't help but put her arms around him, flatten her hands against the ropes of muscle in his back. It seemed as though her entire body, from the tips of her toes to the crown of her scalp, came alive with brand-new and intense sensations. And there was an ache, real and intense, building deep within her. A clawing need to be touched, in a way that no man had ever touched her before.

It was exhilarating and terrifying, and more wonderful than she could have ever imagined.

As though reading her mind, Phillip let one hand slide down her back to cup her behind. He drew her against him, and she could feel that he was just as aroused as she was. And instead of feeling wary or afraid, she felt a need for more. And she longed for the day when she didn't have to tell him no.

Unfortunately, that was not today.

She broke the kiss and pressed her forehead against his shirt, felt that his heart was thumping as hard and fast as her own. And said the only thing she could think to say. "Wow."

A chuckle rumbled through his chest. "Thank you."

She looked up at him, saw that he was smiling. "It's not completely obvious that I have zero experience when it comes to this sort of thing?"

"A little, maybe. But I think that's what I like about you."

"That I'm inexperienced?" She thought men liked women who knew how to please them.

"That you're not afraid to admit it. That you embrace your values, not lean on them. You have no idea how rare that is." He touched her cheek. "Although, I fear your honesty might get you into trouble one of these days."

"My father always told me, nothing bad can come from telling the truth."

"In that case, he would have been very proud of you."

She felt the beginnings of tears prickle in her eyes and laid her head back against his chest, so he wouldn't see. "You think so?"

"I do."

He could really be quite sweet. When he wanted to.

"They're bound to be wondering where we've disappeared to," he said. "We should get back before they dispatch a search party."

Though she would be content to stand here all day, wrapped up in his strong arms, just the two of them, she knew he was right. And as she backed away, she took heart in the fact that today had brought them one step closer to the ideal future that she knew they would have together. Things were falling right into place.

"Let's go," she said.

He reached out and took her hand, laced his fingers through hers and led her out of the woods.

"By the way, I wanted to ask you about something." She told him about the woman who had been staring at her Monday. "She wasn't in any of the profiles. I thought maybe you'd know who she was."

He shrugged. "There were so many people there."

"She would be hard to miss. Long, dark hair, very beautiful. And she never took her eyes off us."

He shook his head. "I'm sorry."

She couldn't shake the feeling that he wasn't being honest with her. He'd been by her side the entire day. Surely he would have noticed someone staring. Wouldn't he? Or maybe, people stared at him all the time.

Besides, what reason did he have to lie? She was probably just being paranoid again.

The walk back to the palace went far too quickly, and when they reached the steps, Phillip's valet was waiting for them.

"An urgent call from the prime minister, sir."

"I'll take it in my office," Phillip told him, then turned to Hannah. "I enjoyed our walk."

He was wearing one of those secret, just-between-us smiles, and it made her feel warm all over.

"Me, too."

"We should do it again soon."

She had a feeling he wasn't talking about the walking part. "I'd like that."

As he started to walk away, Hannah called after him.

"Phillip."

He stopped and turned to her.

"Would you have dinner with me tonight?"

There was a slight hesitation before he said, "I can't."

No explanation, no excuses. No apology.

The sting of disappointment was quick and sharp. Can't, or *won't?* she couldn't help but wonder as he turned and walked away. Why, after they'd had such a good time together, would he not want to be with her? It didn't make sense.

You are not going to let this bother you, she told herself as he disappeared inside, then she walked back over to the blanket where she'd left her things. Only then did she realize that his jacket still hung on her shoulders. But even that couldn't shelter her from the chill that seemed to settle deep in her bones.

They'd taken a huge step forward today. She felt as if they really connected.

Why then, did it feel as though, for every step they took forward, they took two back?

Six

Phillip had just hung up the phone with the prime minister when the door to his office flew open and his sister barged in unannounced.

His secretary stood in the doorway behind her, looking both pained and apologetic. "Princess Sophie to see you, sir."

Even the most loyal of servants were no match against Sophie. Phillip dismissed her with a wave of his hand, and she backed out of the room, closing the door behind her.

"I see you're back," he said.

In lieu of a civilized greeting, she said, "You're an idiot."

Obviously she was in a snit over something. He sighed and leaned back in his chair, curious as to what he had done to provoke her this time, and sure he was about to find out.

"Your fiancée was barely here a day and you took off? To go *hunting?* That was harsh, even for you."

He wasn't even sure why she cared. And because he didn't owe anyone an explanation, least of all her, he didn't give her one.

"She must scare the hell out of you," she said.

Instantly his hackles went up, and before he could stop himself, he warned her, "Don't even go there."

Leave it to Sophie to know exactly which of his buttons to push. From the moment she was born, she had made it her mission in life to torment him, as sisters often did.

"She's the real deal. But you already know that, don't you? That's why you're so determined to keep her at arm's length."

She couldn't be more wrong. He was doing Hannah a favor. But Sophie would never understand that. "You're in no position to give me relationship advice. Who did you run off with the other night, Sophie?"

Her smug smile was all the answer he needed.

"You're coming to a family dinner tomorrow night," she told him. "You and Hannah, at my residence."

"Is that so?"

"It is."

Though he was inclined to refuse, for no reason other than the fact that she demanded it, he realized it was probably a good idea. Were Hannah to befriend Sophie, she might be less unsettled in his absence. She had looked utterly crushed when he refused her dinner invitation. He liked Hannah, and he didn't want her to be unhappy. But he couldn't change the person he was.

"All right," he told Sophie.

She looked surprised. "Really? And here I was all prepared to pull out the brass knuckles."

He would have guessed as much. But, after the heated disagreement he'd just had with the prime minister, he simply wasn't in the mood for another fight. "What time would you like us?"

"Seven o'clock. And bring a bottle of wine. In fact, bring a red and a white. I'm making roast leg of lamb."

"*You're* making it? Well, I'll be sure to bring a bottle of antacid, too. And perhaps I should put the palace physician on high alert as well. Just in case."

Pleased that she had gotten her way, she ignored the jab. Besides, she knew as well as he did that the insult was unfounded. She had trained at one of the most prestigious culinary academies in all of Europe, and was an accomplished, gifted chef. It was a passion that had been vehemently discouraged by their parents. But Sophie somehow always managed to get what she wanted.

It both annoyed and impressed him.

"I'll see you both tomorrow then," she said.

He kept his face bland. "I can hardly contain my excitement."

She only smiled.

"Is that it?" he asked.

"I suppose you noticed Madeline on Monday."

The mystery woman Hannah had asked him about. Of course he'd noticed her. She would have been hard to miss, staring at them the way she had been. "What about her?"

"It would seem she's back to her old tricks."

"Forgive me if don't shudder with fear." Madeline was of no consequence to him or Hannah, which was why he hadn't felt the need to explain who she was. She was nobody.

"You know how she can be. Anything to get attention."

"And confronting her would only feed that need. She'll get bored and find someone else to antagonize."

"She could do some damage in the meantime."

He seriously doubted that. "Is there anything else you needed?"

Sophie shook her head, obviously exasperated with him. "Does your fiancée have the slightest clue how difficult you can be?"

He didn't respond.

"So, I'll see you both tomorrow evening?"

"We'll be there."

She flashed him one of those cryptic, I-know-something-you-don't smiles. One that made him uneasy. Then she was gone.

Forget Madeline. Sophie was the one he should be worried about. This whole dinner scenario seemed a bit too…*domestic* for her taste. Why did he suspect that there was more to this than she was letting on?

Hannah had just finished a quiet dinner alone in her suite, a meal she'd had little appetite for, when Elizabeth knocked on the door.

"You should have left hours ago," Hannah scolded her. She may have been a palace employee, but for heaven's sake, she needed a life of her own outside of work. It seemed as though she was *always* there.

"I was just finishing up a few things," Elizabeth told her. "I was on my way out when a call came in for you."

"Who is it?" She was hoping maybe a friend from back home. God knows she could use a friendly voice right now.

"It's your mother," Elizabeth said, then added, "Again."

This was the fourth call since Hannah left Seattle. Hadn't her mother gotten the message that Hannah wasn't ready to talk to her? She was still too bitter and angry. It was very possible, if Hannah talked to her in her current state of mind, she might say something she would later regret. Like she had the last time they spoke.

"Tell her I'll call her back."

"She said it was urgent."

She would say just about anything to get Hannah's attention. To get her to come to the phone.

"She sounded upset," Elizabeth added.

Hannah felt a slight jerk of alarm. She remembered the last urgent call from her mother. She had been in the university library studying for exams, so engrossed she almost didn't answer her phone, when it buzzed in her pocket. And when she heard her mother's distraught voice, her heart sank.

Sweetheart, you need to come home. Daddy was in an accident….

But he was gone now, and she couldn't imagine anything urgent enough to warrant a return call. "I'll call her tomorrow."

Elizabeth didn't say a word, but she had this look. Not quite disapproval, because a palace employee would never be so bold as to disapprove of anything a royal did or said. It was more the lack of emotion that was giving her away. It was obvious she was trying very hard not to react. Or maybe it was Hannah's own guilty conscience nagging at her. Either way, Hannah knew exactly what she was thinking.

And she was right, of course. "I know, that's what I said yesterday. So technically, today is tomorrow. Right?"

"That is true," Elizabeth agreed.

"You think I should call her, don't you?"

"It's not my place to pass judgment."

Maybe not, but Hannah was pretty sure that's what she was thinking. And the truth was, her mother wasn't likely to stop calling. Not until Hannah gave her the opportunity to apologize for her inappropriate behavior these past few months.

Maybe it would be best, to ease her mother's guilt and Hannah's, if they cleared the air. And besides, it was what Daddy would have wanted. Hannah had always been more like him than her mother. So many times her father had told her, "Your mother isn't like us, Hannah. She's fragile. You just have to be patient."

But sometimes her mother could be so insecure and vulnerable it had been difficult even for her. Not that she was a bad person. She needed constant reassurance that she was loved and appreciated. At times her neediness was utterly exhausting.

"My lady?" Elizabeth was watching her expectantly.

Hannah sighed, knowing what she had to do. Knowing that, for her father's sake, she had to settle this. "I'll talk to her."

"She's on line two," Elizabeth said. Then, ever the proper assistant, nodded and slipped quietly from the room, shutting the door behind her.

Hannah walked over to the phone, hesitating a minute before she finally lifted it off the cradle and pressed the button for line two. "Hello, Mother."

"Oh, Hannah, honey! It's so good to hear your voice!"

Hannah wished she could say the same, but right now the sound of her mother's voice, that syrupy sweetness, was just irritating. "How have you been?"

"Oh, fine. But I've missed you *so* much. I was afraid you wouldn't come to the phone again."

"You said it was urgent."

"How have you been? How do you like it there?"

"Everything is fine here." If she discounted the fact that her fiancé had taken off the minute she arrived. Or that he refused to share dinner with her.

"I've been very busy," she told her mother.

"Is the palace beautiful? And is Phillip as gorgeous as I remember?"

She was stalling. Hannah wished she would just say what she had to say and get it over with. "The palace and Phillip are exactly the same as the last time you saw them. Now, I'd like you to tell me what was so urgent."

"Can't I have a pleasant conversation with my daughter?"

Sadly, no. She had shot any chance of that all to hell with her selfishness. "It's late, and I'm tired."

"Okay, okay." She bubbled with phony laughter. "I'll get to the point."

Thank goodness. Just apologize and get it over with already.

"Now, Hannah, I don't want you to get upset…"

Oh, this was not a good sign. That didn't sound anything like an apology. "Upset about what?"

"I called because I have some good news."

"Okay." Spit it out already.

"Keep December thirtieth open on your calendar."

Oh, no.

"Why?" she forced herself to ask, even though she already suspected what was coming next.

Dreaded it, in fact.

"Because I'm getting married!"

"Married?"

"Now, honey, I know what you're thinking—"

"Daddy has been gone barely a year!"

"Hannah, please, you're not being fair."

"Fair?"

"A year is a long time when you're alone."

It was the same song and dance she'd fed Hannah three months after his death, when she'd gone out on her first date. *I'm lonely,* she'd told Hannah. What she didn't seem to get is that she had just lost her husband, therefore she was *supposed* to be lonely. She was supposed to mourn his death, not take the first opportunity to run out and find a replacement.

"Please don't be angry, Hannah."

"Who is he?"

"No one you know. He owns a small law firm outside of Seattle. But you'll love him, honey."

No, she wouldn't. No one could replace her father. *Ever.* And if her mother honestly believed someone could, she was more oblivious than Hannah could have imagined.

"I was thinking, I could bring him to your wedding. So you could meet him."

She didn't want to meet him. "For security reasons, that won't be possible."

"Please give him a chance. He's such a sweet, generous man. And he loves me."

Hannah was sure that what he probably loved was the substantial estate her father had left behind. "You say that like Daddy *didn't* love you. Or is it that you didn't love him?"

"That's unfair. You know that I loved your father very much." There was a quiver in her voice that said she was on the verge of tears. No big surprise there. She often used tears to win sympathy. But Hannah wasn't buying it this time.

"Then why are you so eager to replace him?"

"You've gone on with your life. I should be allowed to go on with my life, too."

It wasn't the same thing and she knew it. Besides, Hannah wasn't out trying to find a new father, was she? "And so you have, Mom. You don't need my permission."

"No, but I would like your blessing."

"I really need to go now."

"Hannah, please—"

"We'll talk about this when you're here next week," she said.

"I love you, honey."

"Goodbye, Mom." She could hear her mother still talking as she set the phone back in the cradle. But if she stayed on the line any longer, she would have wound up saying something she regretted.

There was nothing she could do or say to change her mother's mind. She had obviously made her decision. And since Hannah had no control over the situation, there was no point in wasting her time worrying about it.

She had other things to keep her occupied. Wedding plans and redecorating, and hours of reading to do. She didn't need her mother anymore.

She sat on the sofa, surrounded with binders full of information to read, color swatches and wallpaper samples to choose from, last-minute wedding plans to tie up. But she couldn't seem to work up the enthusiasm for any of it.

She felt too...*edgy.*

Hannah decided a long, hot bath with her lavender bath gel might relax her. Afterward she towel-dried her hair and changed into her most comfortable cotton pajamas. She curled up in bed to watch television, browsing past the gazillion channels available, but there wasn't a thing on that held her interest.

She snapped the television off and tossed the remote on the coverlet. She was bored silly, yet she didn't feel like doing anything.

Hannah glanced over at the closet door, where Phillip's jacket hung. She had planned to give it back to him tomorrow. But what if he'd forgotten he'd lent it to her, and was wondering where he'd left it.

Yeah right. She just wanted an excuse to see him. Which in itself was silly because he was her fiancé. She shouldn't *need* an excuse to see him. Right? If she wanted to see him, she should just...*see him.* Shouldn't she?

Yes, she decided. She should.

Before she lost her nerve, she rolled out of bed and grabbed her robe, shoving her arms in the sleeves and belting it securely at her waist. She stuck her feet in her slippers, grabbed Phillip's jacket, and headed out into the hall.

His suite was all the way down the main hall at the opposite end of the east wing. She had never actually been there, but it had been part of the tour Elizabeth took her on earlier in the week.

When she reached his door, she lifted her hand to knock, then hesitated, drawing it back.

What was she *doing?* Begging for his attention? Was she really so pathetic? Had she so little pride? Wasn't she stronger than that?

She turned to walk back the way she came from, but hesitated again.

On second thought, why shouldn't she stop by to give him his jacket? He was her fiancé, wasn't he? And damn it, she had worked hard to prepare herself for her role as his wife. Didn't she deserve a little something in return? Was a little bit of his time really all that much to ask for?

No, she decided, it definitely was not.

She turned back, and before she could talk herself out of it again, rapped hard on the door.

Seven

Get a grip, Hannah, she told herself, since her heart was about to pound clear through her chest. It's not like he's naked.

But darn close.

A pair of Egyptian cotton pajama bottoms rode low on Phillip's hips as he opened the door. Other than that, all she was able to comprehend, to process, was the ridiculous amount of muscle she was seeing.

Wide, ripped shoulders and bulging biceps. Lean hips and toned, defined abs. And she could only imagine what was under the pajamas. In fact, she *was* imagining it.

She was so stunned silly by his perfect physique, it took a moment to register that he was speaking to her.

She peeled her eyes from his flawless pecks, located his face, and uttered a very eloquent, "Huh?"

Amusement danced in the depth of his eyes. "I said, is there something wrong?"

"Wrong?"

"Why are you here?"

Think, Hannah. Why did you come all the way down here? Then she remembered the jacket still hanging from her left hand. "No. Nothing is wrong. I just wanted to give this back to you."

She held the jacket out to him, and he took it.

"Is that it?" he asked.

"Yes." She shook her head. "No."

He leaned in the door frame, arms folded across his chest, waiting patiently for her to elaborate. And, boy, were his biceps *huge.* So thick and strong look-ing, like he could probably bench-press a compact car and not break a sweat.

Did it suddenly get a lot hotter in here? Her cheeks were on fire and she was feeling just a little light-headed.

What was wrong with her? It wasn't as if she had never seen a half-naked man before.

The biggest problem here wasn't that she was wary of what she was seeing. Instead, she felt a very real and intense desire—no, not desire, *need*—to put her hands all over him.

She locked them together behind her back. Just to be safe.

"Are you all right?" he asked, though he looked more amused than concerned.

"Yes. I just…" She shook her head again. "No. I'm not."

"Maybe you should come in." He opened the door wider and stepped aside.

You know you shouldn't be doing this, she told herself. Their wedding was still more than a week away. It was one thing to flirt and steal a kiss here and there, but going into his suite, at this late hour. In her *pajamas*. And Phillip almost naked.

She was really pushing it.

So you just won't let anything happen, she decided. It's not as though she was a slave to her libido.

She had waited this long. She could wait a little while longer.

But the question was, could Phillip? And if he took matters into his own hands, would she find the strength to stop him?

Bad idea or not, she followed him inside. His sitting room was much larger than her own, and closer to the size of the one they would be moving into after the wedding. And it was undeniably masculine. Dark polished wood and dark patterned fabric in rich hues. But not so dark that it was dreary or threatening. In contrast, the effect was warm and welcoming.

"This is nice," she said, ideas popping into her head of how she might incorporate both his and her individual styles to create a decor they could both be comfortable in.

See, she told herself, coming here was a good thing.

"So, what's up?" he asked.

She turned to him, with every intention of meeting his eyes, but her gaze kept snagging slightly lower.

"Hannah?"

She pried her eyes from his torso and met his gaze. He was grinning again.

"If it would help get the conversation rolling, I could put on a shirt."

Though she knew he was only teasing, her cheeks flamed with embarrassment. "Sorry."

"No apology necessary. I'm flattered. But maybe you should tell me what's wrong."

"Wrong?"

"I asked if you were okay, and you said no."

Had she? My goodness, he must have thought she was a total ditz. Now that she was here, she had no idea what to say to him. So she blurted out the first thing that came to mind. "My mother called."

He didn't seem to get the significance. "Is *she* okay?"

"She's fine, she just…" Her voice cracked, and she realized, with horror, that tears burned the corners of her eyes. What was *wrong* with her? She was not a crier. She was tougher than that. Besides, she wasn't that upset. More angry than sad.

"She just what?" he asked.

"She's—" A half hiccup, half sob, worked its way up her throat and she battled to swallow it back down. "She's getting married."

Despite her resolve, the instant the words left her lips, the tears welled up over the edges of her lids and rolled down her cheeks. Mortified, she covered her face with her hands.

What was wrong with her? She should be spitting mad, not blubbering like a baby.

Then she felt Phillip's arms go around her, draw her against him, and something inside her seemed to snap. Every bit of tension and anger that had built inside her let go in a limb-weakening rush and she all but melted against him.

"You think it's too soon?" he asked. "For your mother to remarry, I mean."

Because she wasn't sure her voice was steady enough for a verbal reply, she nodded.

"Do you want to talk about it?"

She shook her head. Just knowing he was there for her if she needed him was enough right now.

He didn't say anything else. He just held her and stroked her hair. She held on tight, her face pressed to his warm, bare skin, and concentrated on taking slow, deep breaths, until she felt the tears begin to work their way back down. Apparently, this was exactly what she'd needed. How did he always seem to know exactly what to do and say to make her feel better?

"You okay?" he asked.

She nodded. "I'm sorry."

"Sorry for what?"

"For barging in on you like this. And getting all wishy-washy and emotional."

"It's okay."

"I don't usually do this. I'm not a crier. It…it's just been a really stressful couple of days."

"I can imagine."

"Bringing the jacket back was just an excuse," she admitted, and could swear she felt him smile.

"I know."

She looked up at him. Of all the women in the world that he could have had, why did he pick her? "I guess I just… I guess I was lonely."

He touched her cheek, brushing away the last remnants of the tears with his thumb.

"All day I have appointments and meetings, and sometimes I just can't wait to be alone, to have a minute to myself. But then, when I'm finally alone, I feel so...isolated. Does that make sense?"

"Trust me, I know exactly what you mean. And you get used to it. I promise."

Maybe she didn't want to get used to it. She wanted them to be a regular family. She wanted it so bad she ached deep in her heart.

"I was going to wait until tomorrow to tell you this," he said. "My sister invited us to dinner at her residence tomorrow evening."

"Really?"

"I hope you don't mind, but I told her we would be there."

Mind? She was absolutely ecstatic. They would *finally* share a meal together. Like a *real* family. Not to mention that she had been eager to get to know her future sister-in-law. "I would love to."

She was so happy, she nearly burst into tears again. Instead, she rose up on her toes and kissed him. Just a quick, sweet kind of kiss, so he would know how much it meant to her.

But it felt so nice, so...*perfect,* she kissed him again. This one lasting just a little longer than the first. She felt his arms tighten around her, the flex of his back where her hands rested.

And because the second one was even better than the first, she kissed him again.

And *again*.

And then she couldn't stop.

Phillip had Hannah exactly where he wanted her. Her body pressed against him, her arms circling his neck, hands tangled in his hair. And her mouth—damn, what she could do with her mouth. He had never been with a woman who kissed so…earnestly.

He could have her tonight if he wanted, *before* the wedding, just as he'd planned. So, why did it feel wrong? As if he were somehow betraying her trust?

Since when did he care about anyone but himself?

He wouldn't be having this problem, this case of an overactive conscience, if she wasn't so damned honest all the time. If she didn't walk around with her heart on her sleeve.

He'd told her, just this afternoon, that her honesty would get her into trouble, and she insisted that honesty was a good thing. Well, it was looking like maybe she was right.

Yet here he was, kissing her, touching her, when what he should be doing was telling her no. But, damn, she felt good.

Maybe she didn't understand the consequences of her actions. Maybe if he pushed just a little further, tempted her just a little bit more, she would realize what she was doing and put on the brakes.

Maybe he could *make* her tell him no.

He let his hand slide down her back, slowly. Over the dip of her waist, the curve of her hip. Then he went lower, cupping the soft swell of her behind. She whimpered softly, but didn't attempt to pull away. He took it one step further, pulling her against him, so she would feel exactly what all of this fooling around was doing to him. And, hell, she felt amazing. All soft and warm and sweet smelling. And rather than deter her, his actions seemed only to fuel her determination.

She drew her nails across his skin, arched and rubbed herself against him, and he couldn't stop the husky sound of need that welled up from his chest.

She had given every indication that she was a virgin, but now he wasn't so sure. And he didn't know how he felt about that. He liked the idea that she would be his alone.

Her hands were on his shoulders, his chest, traveling slowly downward, in the direction of his waistband. A few more inches, and he wouldn't be able to stop.

Virgin or not, how could he, in good conscience, deny Hannah what she told him she wanted—the privilege of waiting for her wedding day?

The truth of the matter was, as good as this felt, as much as she seemed to want this, he couldn't.

He broke the kiss and backed away, leaving her flush and out of breath. And honestly, he wasn't faring much better. "We have to stop."

Her cheeks were red, her voice husky with desire. "Why?"

"Because you don't want this."

"Yes, I do. I want us to make love."

She tried to kiss him again, to touch him, but he manacled her wrists in his hands. "No, you don't. You're upset, and it's affecting your judgment."

"I'm not upset. Honestly."

"Hannah, if we let this happen, you'll regret it."

"I won't."

"It's only a week." He could hardly believe what he was saying. That he was the one talking *her* out of sex. He must have been completely out of his mind.

Her expression said she was thinking the same thing. "Today, next week. What's the difference?"

"You don't mean that."

"Phillip, I want this. Tonight. Right now."

She tugged against his grip, but he didn't let go. She could beg and cajole until she was blue, and he still wouldn't change his mind. And the worst part was that this was all his fault. He had driven her to this by shutting her out of his life.

He'd thought that, by keeping her at a distance, he was doing her a favor. So she wouldn't get too attached. He could see now that he was only making her miserable. She had left everything familiar to move to a strange country with people she didn't know, and he'd welcomed her by shutting her out. It's a wonder she hadn't packed up and headed back to America.

Sophie was right. He was an idiot.

At the risk of hurting her feelings yet again, he said the only thing he could to get his point across. "Maybe you want it, but I *don't.*"

Phillip's words splashed over her like a bucket of ice water. Was he actually telling her *no?* He was a man, and didn't all men inherently want sex? She thought he would jump at the chance.

He let go of her wrists and she took an unsteady step backward. "You're serious?"

"Believe me when I say, I'm just as surprised as you are."

This didn't make sense. He was turned on. All she had to do was look at the front of his pajamas and she could *see* how aroused he was. Why didn't he want her? "Did I do something wrong?"

"Oh, no. You did everything right."

"Then, why?"

He shook his head, dragged a hand through his hair. "I respect you too much to let you do this."

She was so stunned, it took a second for the meaning of his words to sink in.

It was probably one of the sweetest, most wonderful things anyone had ever said to her.

And he was right. If they had made love tonight, she would have regretted it. She was feeling emotional and upset, and she was letting it cloud her judgment.

She wanted to feel close to someone. And she just naturally assumed that, by sleeping with him, she would bring them closer together. But as important as sex was in a relationship, it was still just sex. The other stuff mattered a whole lot more.

Like the fact that he cared enough about her to stop her from making the biggest mistake of her life. What more could she possibly ask for?

"Waiting one more week isn't going to kill us," he said. "Is it?"

She bit her lip and shook her head. Not after waiting twenty-six years. And she didn't miss the irony that it had been her saying the exact same thing to him less than a week ago. "I'm sorry. I don't know what I was thinking."

"You have nothing to be sorry about. I should be more attentive."

"You're busy. I understand that."

"But not so busy that I can't have dinner with my fiancée occasionally."

He touched her hair, brushing it back from her face. "So much has been expected of you, but you've received little in return."

The last thing she wanted was for him to think she was ungrateful. "I'm well aware of the fact that my position will require a certain amount of sacrifice."

"I'm just not used to sharing my time," he admitted.

Or his feelings, she was guessing. And considering the environment he was raised in, it's no wonder. With a mother that cold, and a father whose mistresses were common knowledge, who wouldn't grow up learning to hide their emotions?

But she knew with time she would be able to draw him out of his shell. She would make him see that it was okay to trust his feelings, to let his guard down. It would just take time.

"I'll try not to be overly demanding," she said. Like her mother could often be. "I'll try to give you the space you need." Phillip nodded, although she couldn't help noticing he made no promises in return.

She could see that making this marriage work was going to be a lot harder than she anticipated.

Eight

Phillip knocked on the door to her suite at exactly 6:45 p.m., just as he'd promised last night before she left his room.

When she opened the door and he stepped into her sitting room, she breathed a soft sigh of appreciation. As always, he looked perfect. Dark wool slacks that fit him just right, a long-sleeved, cashmere pullover sweater the same rich, smoky gray as his eyes, topped with a stately jacket.

"I'm just about ready," she told him.

He eyed her with obvious appreciation. "You look beautiful."

The compliment, the way his eyes swept so leisurely over her, left her feeling warm and fuzzy. The extra time she'd taken to blow her hair out smooth and straight, the care she had taken on her makeup, and her choice of dress—a red, clingy number that was sexy, without being too flashy or risqué—had been worth the effort.

"I'd have been ready sooner," she told him, "but my meeting with the wedding planner ran longer than I anticipated."

"No rush," he said. "I doubt she'll start without us."

Still, she hated to be late for anything. "I just have to grab my shoes and a sweater."

She scurried into her room to her closet. She yanked her cardigan from the hanger and grabbed a pair of sling-back, marginally sexy heels from the top shelf. Her totally impractical, just-for-fun shoes.

"How are the wedding plans going?" he called from the sitting room. And because she was sure he was only asking to be polite, she didn't embellish. The important thing was that he was making an effort.

"Very well," she called back, tugging the shoes on her feet. "Did you have a productive day?"

"Not really."

His voice was close. She turned and saw that he was leaning in the bedroom doorway, watching her.

"Did I mention how beautiful you look?"

"I believe you did."

He was wearing that hungry, I'm-going-to-eat-you-alive expression. Like the one he wore last night. And when she remembered what it felt like to touch him, to put her hands on his bare skin, she started to get a funny tickle in the pit of her stomach.

Exactly one more week until the wedding. This time next Friday, they would be legally married and probably at their reception. And after that, either his or her bedroom....

This week couldn't go by fast enough.

"I'm ready," she said.

"There's a car waiting." He stepped aside so she could exit the bedroom, but as she was walking past, he curled a hand around her upper arm, tugged her to him and kissed her. A deep, toe-curling, out-of-this-world kiss that she felt from her toes to her scalp and everywhere along the way. And it was over way too fast.

"What was that for?"

He grinned down at her. "Do I need a reason?"

Heck no.

But if he kept doing stuff like that, looking at her like a hungry wolf, this was going to be the longest week of her life.

The car dropped Hannah and Phillip at Sophie's residence. When they knocked, a butler answered the door. He nodded and motioned them inside, just as Sophie swept into the foyer.

She wore a flowing, gauzy dress that complimented her long, willowy figure. She wore her long, dark hair up and off her face. She looked utterly elegant, if you overlooked the fact that she was barefoot.

"You're right on time!" She pulled Hannah into a warm embrace and kissed her cheek. She smelled of honeysuckle and faintly of apples. Then she stepped back and looked them both up and down. "Aren't you two the handsome couple."

Phillip handed her the bottles of wine. "I hope these will do."

She read the labels, then flashed him a bright smile. "Perfect."

She passed them along to the butler. "Would either of you like a drink before dinner?"

Hannah shook her head. "No, thank you."

"Me neither," Phillip said. "Unless you think I might *need* a drink."

She smiled sweetly, but with just a hint of sass. "Why would I think that?"

There was something going on, Hannah could feel it. Sophie was up to something. Or at least, Phillip suspected she was.

"Dinner will be a few minutes yet. Why don't we wait in the study?"

Her residence was as richly decorated and furnished as the palace. More modern, but just as warm and inviting. And the scents coming from the kitchen were mouthwatering.

"Your house is beautiful," Hannah told her.

"Thank you, Hannah. After dinner I can give you the full tour."

"I'd like that."

As they entered the study, Hannah was so busy taking in the interior that, only when she felt Phillip go board stiff beside her, did she realize something was wrong.

She followed his line of sight and realized there was someone else in the room with them. For a second she was confused, then she recognized the man sitting in the winged leather chair across the room.

The family resemblance was undeniable.

"What's the meaning of this?" Philip demanded. Hannah actually took a step aside, so she wouldn't get caught in the crosshairs. "You never said *he* would be coming."

Sophie shrugged. "You never asked."

Phillip's half brother rose from his seat and shot Sophie a stern look. "I'm a bit surprised myself."

"I knew you were up to something," Phillip told his sister. "But I never imagined you would pull something like this."

He looked seconds from blowing his top. Hannah wouldn't have been at all surprised if steam shot from his ears. She had never seen Phillip this way and, frankly, it intimidated as much as fascinated her. She was just happy that the animosity he shot like laser beams from his charcoal eyes wasn't directed her way.

Sophie, on the other hand, didn't look the least bit rattled. The glare Phillip shot her would have crushed the average person, but she didn't even flinch.

She had probably seen it so many times, she was immune.

"I invited you over for a family dinner. And we're all family, aren't we?" She turned to Hannah. "I don't believe you've met our brother."

Hannah didn't miss the fact that she said *brother*, not *half brother*. "No, I haven't."

"Hannah, this is Ethan Rafferty. Ethan, this is Phillip's fiancée, Hannah Renault."

Hannah stepped forward and shook his hand. His grip was firm and unashamed.

"It's a pleasure, Hannah." He spoke with a very distinct American accent, and though it was silly, she couldn't help liking him instantly.

She had seen photos of him in the paper and always thought he bore a resemblance to Phillip, but in person, the similarities were striking. They were built similarly, even though Ethan wasn't as tall, and their coloring was the same. Intense smoky-gray eyes and dark hair, although, while Phillip's was short and wavy, Ethan's hung long and straight to his shoulders.

They also wore identical angry expressions.

Hannah had the distinct impression that this was not going to be the pleasant family dinner she had been hoping for.

"We're leaving," Phillip said.

"Great idea," Ethan replied.

Sophie rolled her eyes. "Oh, for heaven's sake, you two are acting like spoiled children. *Grow up,* already."

They refocused their glare from each other to their sister. They looked so much alike, it gave Hannah chills. If only they could see themselves. But Hannah was sure neither would be able to see past their pre-conceived notions of one another.

And though Hannah was inclined to agree with Sophie, and would have happily backed her, she was still an outsider. It wasn't her place to interfere with family issues. Besides, she didn't have siblings, much less illegitimate ones, so how could she begin to under-stand the complicated relationship they must have?

"Glare at me all you like," Sophie told them. "Whether you like it or not, you two are related. So just deal with it." With a frustrated huff, she turned to the door. "What is it, Wilson?"

Hannah turned to see that the butler was standing in the doorway.

"Dinner is served, miss."

Sophie turned back to her brothers. "Is one civilized meal together really too much to ask for? Can't we put aside our differences, forget the past for one night and *try* to get along like mature adults?"

Hannah could see, by both men's expressions, that she had hit a nerve. After a moment, they both grumbled an agreement.

"Thank you." Sophie led them all to the dining room, and had the good sense to seat the men on opposite sides of the table.

The food was beyond fantastic, each course more delectable than the next. The conversation however was pathetically lacking. Though Sophie tried to start a dialogue, extracting more than a one-word answer from either of them was like pulling wisdom teeth with a pair of tweezers. Despite what Phillip had told Hannah about Sophie being a free spirit, it was clear that she cared very deeply for both her brothers, and wanted to see them acting like a family.

"Everything was delicious," Hannah told Sophie as the dessert dishes were being cleared.

Sophie smiled. "Thank you, Hannah. I don't get in the kitchen nearly as much as I'd like these days. It's nice to know that I haven't lost my touch."

Sophie made dinner? "I didn't know you cook."

"Sophie is an amazing chef," Ethan said, an undeniable note of pride in his voice. "She studied in France. I offered her a position as head chef in the resort of her choosing, but she turned me down."

Phillip shot him a look, one that said he'd heard nothing of the job offer, and didn't like being left out of the loop. "Sophie's place is here, with her family."

At first, Hannah thought he was just being stubborn, then she realized he was jealous. After all, she was the only immediate family he had left. If she moved away, he would be alone.

But if he could care so deeply for one sibling, surely he could find room in his heart for one more. Did it really matter so much that he and Ethan shared only one parent?

"Until he agreed that opening one here on Morgan Isle would be the perfect compromise," Sophie said. "Speaking of that, Phillip, did you read the proposal I left on your desk?"

"I may have skimmed it," he said.

Phillip hadn't mentioned a business proposal to Hannah. Of course, he wasn't exactly chatty when it came to the professional aspects of his life. Or any part of his life, for that matter.

Picking up on Hannah's confusion, Sophie said,

"I've proposed a business partnership between Ethan and the rest of the family."

"And why is it he needs a new business partner?" Phillip asked.

Ethan shot daggers with his eyes, so Hannah was guessing the reason was an unpleasant one.

Sophie only smiled. "If that's the way you want to play this, I'd be happy to quote a list of each and every one of your mistakes and transgressions, Phillip."

Phillip glared silently at her, and Ethan actually smiled. No doubt about it, Sophie was the driving force in this family. She pulled the strings.

"Here's the thing," Sophie told Phillip, leaning toward him to emphasize her point. "I want this. But I can't do it without you."

"So, what's in it for me?" Phillip asked.

"Besides the money? You've complained incessantly, for as long as I can remember, that I need to embrace my position in this family. Well, if you agree to this partnership, you'll never hear a complaint from me again."

She definitely had Phillip's attention. "How do I know you'll live up to that?"

"Have I ever lied to you?"

Hannah could see by his expression that she hadn't.

"Well?" she asked. "Are you in or out?"

"I need time to think about it."

"No. You've had months to think about it. I want an answer tonight." She turned to Hannah. "I think the boys need a few minutes to talk. How about that tour I promised you?"

Sophie led Hannah to the study, where she poured herself a tumbler of scotch. She offered Hannah a glass, but she shook her head.

Sophie took a long sip. Then she took a deep breath and asked, "So, how did I do in there?"

Hannah realized that, although Sophie seemed to be in complete control, the experience had really taken a toll on her. "You were great. It was impressive how you kept them both in line."

"Years of practice, believe me. I've never known two more stubborn men in my life. Though they would die before acknowledging it, they're so much alike."

"I noticed that."

"And I love them both to death, even though they don't always make it easy."

"Tell me if I'm overstepping my bounds, but what did Phillip mean when he asked why Ethan needs a new partner?"

"Ethan's former business partner recently embezzled several million then disappeared. He risks losing everything. And it's not like any of that money was handed to him either. He started with nothing and built his empire from the ground up, one brick at a time."

Hannah shook her head. "How awful."

"I was the one who suggested the partnership. At first he wouldn't hear about it. He was too proud to accept what he considered a handout. But as it stands now, he doesn't have much choice. When our lawyers came up with a business proposal, and it was clear that it was a partnership and not charity, he finally gave in." She took another sip of her drink. "Phillip, I wasn't so sure about. We've been going back and forth with this for months."

"I think he'll go for it."

Sophie smiled. "I like you, Hannah. I think you'll be good for Phillip. I just hope you realize what you're getting yourself into, marrying my brother."

"I've been preparing for this for eight years."

Her eyes widened. "Seriously?"

She nodded. "I had tutors and coaches and advisors."

Sophie shook her head in disbelief. "Wow. And you think you're ready?"

She sure hope so. "I guess we'll see."

"The 'rents tried to handpick a spouse for me, too. He was a duke. Not bad looking, but he had the personality of a brick."

"I take it that didn't go over well."

She shook her head. "If I ever get married, it will be to someone I love. Not that I'm knocking what you and Phillip are doing," she quickly added.

"You wouldn't be the first. My friends thought it was really cool at first. I mean, who wouldn't want to marry a prince and live in a palace? It's every girl's fantasy. Then they saw me spending my weekends in the dorm studying while they went out and had fun. They all had boyfriends, and I was always alone. When they realized how much work it really was, they all thought I was crazy."

"It's kind of ironic. You spent years training for a life that I couldn't get far enough away from."

"Yes, but I wasn't forced into this life. It was my choice."

"Was it?"

She nodded. Though raised in the U.S., her father was born on Morgan Isle. A cousin to a cousin of the royal family. It was the only reason she was chosen to be Phillip's wife. Something about maintaining the royal bloodlines.

"There is one thing I never learned," she told Sophie. "Cooking."

"You don't cook at all?"

"The most complicated thing I've ever made was boxed macaroni and cheese."

Sophie made a sour face. "That sounds dreadful."

"But I've always wanted to learn."

"I could teach you," Sophie said.

"Would you really?"

"Of course! I would love to."

"Okay," Hannah said, feeling suddenly and inexplicably happy. Not only would she have a sister, something she had yearned for as long as she could remember, but it looked as though she had made a friend.

"Now, how about that tour I promised?" Sophie said.

Though Hannah's life here started out a bit rocky, it seemed that things were taking a turn for the better.

Nine

It was after eleven o'clock when Phillip and Hannah returned to the palace. And most of that time he and Ethan spent holed up in the dining room discussing the proposed partnership. On the ride back, Hannah asked how it had gone and got a noncommittal shrug, but *something* must have gone right. When all was said and done, Phillip agreed to the proposal. Already plans were being made for him to tour several of the resort sites.

In fact, he would leave Sunday morning and wouldn't return until Thursday evening, less than twenty-four hours before their nuptials.

"Does that upset you?" Phillip had asked her as they walked up to her suite.

She shook her head. It was business. And important. Besides, it was bad luck for the bride and groom to see each other right before the wedding. This would remove any temptation.

"It will make seeing each other on our wedding day that much more special," she said. And that made him smile.

They reached her door, and though she'd planned to tell him good-night, kiss him and go inside alone, he asked, "Are you going to invite me in for a nightcap?"

It would probably be better if she didn't, but it had turned out to be such a nice night, she hated to see it end just yet. "Can you promise to behave?"

He grinned. "Can you?"

God, she loved it when he teased her.

She opened the door. "Phillip, would you like to come in for a nightcap?"

"I would love to." He followed her inside, shutting the door behind them.

Alone again. Five days ago she would have been a nervous wreck. Now she looked forward to the times they spent, just the two of them.

The room was dim, the only light from a small lamp in one corner of the room. She reached for the light switch by the door, but he intercepted her hand.

"I prefer it darker, if you don't mind." When she shot him a questioning look, he grinned and added, "Didn't I tell you, I'm part vampire?"

If that was true, he could bite her neck anytime.

He crossed to the wet bar. "Brandy?"

"That sounds good."

He poured two brandies while she took off her shoes and sweater.

Phillip sat on the sofa and when she sat down beside him, he looped an arm around her shoulder, drawing her close. For several minutes they just sat there, sipping their drinks in companionable silence. He was a warm, solid presence beside her, the stubble on his chin rough against her forehead. And he smelled so good. So…familiar.

Yet there was still so much about him she didn't know. And that was okay, she realized. At first, she thought they should know one another completely before the wedding. Now she liked the idea of getting to know him gradually.

She set her drink down and curled closer, drawing her knees up and resting them over the tops of his thighs. She closed her eyes and laid her head on his chest, taking it all in. The way he felt, the way he smelled, the thump of his pulse against her cheek. The way his arms felt around her, the sensation that she was and would always be safe there.

She stored every second of it in her memory, so that when he was gone, she wouldn't miss him as much. Or, who knows, maybe it would make her miss him even more.

After a while he gave her a little nudge. "Are you falling asleep on me?"

"Just thinking."

"About what?"

"How many times I imagined us like this. What it would feel like."

"How does it feel?"

She wrapped both arms around him and squeezed, feeling sleepy and content. "Wonderful. Perfect."

He set his glass down beside hers. "Is that all you imagined?"

She grinned up at him, knowing exactly what he was suggesting. "Usually we were kissing."

He cupped her chin and raised her face to his, brushed his lips across hers, and a purr of pleasure curled in her throat.

He lifted his head and looked down at her. "Like that?"

"Hmmm, just like that."

He lowered his head and kissed her again, deeper this time. And longer. And she could feel herself beginning to melt. But something was different this time. As much as she wanted him, wanted to be close, she didn't feel the urgency that was usually there. That soul-deep ache that seemed to push them too far, too fast.

Phillip must have felt the same way, because he took it slow. Kissing, touching. And she couldn't get over how right it felt. The way they seemed to fit, to be completely in sync.

She wasn't sure how much time had passed, but after a while he whispered against her lips, "It's late. I should go."

She pressed her cheek against his chest, felt his arms tighten around her. "I wish you could stay."

"It won't be long before I can."

Reluctantly she uncurled herself from around him and climbed from his lap. He rose to his feet and offered a hand to help her up. At the door, he kissed her again, but what was meant to be a quick goodbye peck progressed to another ten minutes of kissing and touching.

When he finally pulled away, they were both a bit breathless.

"I really have to go," he said. "I have a busy day tomorrow. And I'm sure you do, too."

He was right. She let her arms fall from around his neck and backed away from the temptation. "Is there any way you could spare a few minutes tomorrow afternoon? The decorator will be here and I could show you the plans for the suite. I want to know what you think."

"You're free to do whatever you'd like."

She appreciated his trust in her, but what she would appreciate more was his input. "I want to be sure you like it, too."

He shrugged. "If it's that important to you."

"It is."

"All right. I suppose, if the designer is adequate, it might be time that I redecorate my own suite."

It took a second for his words to sink in, and a few more for their meaning to register. Then it made sense. She suddenly knew exactly why he didn't care what she did with the suite. And it had nothing to do with trusting her taste.

It was of no consequence to him, because he wasn't going to be living there.

There was something wrong.

Phillip could feel it. He could see it written clearly on Hannah's face. Although for the life of him, he had no idea what it could be.

He had done everything right tonight. And, with the exception of the stunt Sophie pulled at dinner, it hadn't been nearly as trying as he'd anticipated. In fact, being with Hannah wasn't a hardship at all. He enjoyed her company.

Yet, as hard as he'd tried, she was *still* unhappy.

"What did I do?" he asked.

She blinked rapidly, as though surprised by his question. "Wh-what do you mean?"

Did she honestly think him so daft or self-centered that he wouldn't notice when she was upset? "You have that look," he said. "And I have the distinct impression I did or said something wrong."

She shook her head, too emphatically to be believable, and plastered a smile on her face. "No. Of course not."

He sighed. "Hannah, you're a terrible liar."

She bit her lip and lowered her eyes.

She wasn't going to make this easy. She was going to make him drag it out of her. As long as he lived, he would never understand the inner workings of the female mind.

Fine then, if that was what she wanted. "Just tell me why you're upset."

"It's really late, and I'm exhausted," she said, but she wouldn't look him in the eye.

He folded his arms across his chest. "I'm not leaving until you tell me what's wrong."

She glanced up at him, saw that he was serious. That he really wasn't going anywhere. "It's stupid."

"Go on."

"I thought… I just assumed…"

He waited patiently for her to continue.

She looked down at her hands, clenched in front of her, and said softly, "I thought that, after the wedding, we would be sharing a suite."

He wasn't sure what surprised him more, that she would want to share a suite, or that it upset her that they wouldn't. Honestly, it had never crossed his mind. His parents had been married, yet they never shared living quarters. Maybe in her world, that was what married couples did.

But this was not going to be a typical marriage. She knew that going in and he wasn't about to change his ways. "Hannah—"

"It's okay. Really."

Obviously it was not okay. He could see that she was trying to be tough, but her voice had that wobbly sound she got just before she cried. He was sorry she was hurt, but this was not negotiable. "This is the way things are. My parents conducted their marriage the same way and I intend to follow those rules."

"I understand," she said. But he could see that she didn't. She was hurt and confused.

"I thought you knew coming into this that it was an arrangement. I'm sorry if this upsets you or you were misled about my intentions." Hadn't they determined, on more than one occasion, that he was the king, and he made the rules?

But that had been in jest. There was nothing funny about this.

She sniffled softly and swiped at her cheek. "I'm well aware of our arrangements. Just forget I said anything."

It pained him to see her so distraught, and trying so hard to hide it. He wanted to say something, anything, to make her feel better, but the words escaped him. How did she manage, without even trying, to make him feel so helpless?

So…inadequate?

She took a deep breath and blew it out. "I'm sorry. I'm just tired." She flashed him a smile that almost looked genuine. "I'm up way past my bedtime. Not to mention that it's been a really crazy week."

That it had. Both of their lives had been changed dramatically, but he had to remind himself that hers bore the brunt of it. It was just going to take time for them to adjust. And would it kill him to spare her just a little bit more of his time? At least until she settled in.

"Do you have plans for lunch tomorrow?" he asked.

"Nothing I can't change."

He had a ridiculously busy schedule, but he could spare some time if it kept the peace. "We could eat, then take a walk in the garden."

Her smile grew. "I would love to."

Though he felt ridiculous for it, the happiness that filled her eyes warmed his heart. "One o'clock?"

She nodded vigorously.

"It's a date then." He pressed one last lingering kiss to her lips, then opened the door. "I'll see you tomorrow."

"See you tomorrow," she said, before she closed the door behind him.

And as he walked to his own suite, he considered the events of the past week, since the minute she stepped out of that car and into his life. He knew she had prepared for her position as his wife, and it was clear she took it very seriously. It was her motivation that had him puzzled. Until she moved to Morgan Isle, he had been sure she'd done it for the title. For the security of her family. Yet she seemed to have every intention of making this marriage work.

She seemed to want the real thing.

But that was more than he was willing, or *capable,* of giving.

Friday came faster than Hannah could have imagined. Faster than she was ready for. She'd spent the past eight years preparing for this, and suddenly everything was happening so fast, she barely had time to catch her breath. And though she vowed not to let the living arrangements upset her, it had been in the back of her mind.

She was beginning to suspect that her ideas about her perfect life with Phillip, all her carefully mapped plans, were silly and immature. And for the most part, totally unrealistic.

She of all people should understand that life didn't follow a plan. If it did, she never would have lost her father, and her mother wouldn't be trying to replace him. She couldn't expect Phillip to fall into line and live his life, one she knew virtually nothing about, by her preconceived notion of what a marriage was *supposed* to be.

But even if things didn't go exactly as she planned, that didn't mean she and Phillip wouldn't be happy. It was just going to take time to figure things out, to get them running smoothly, and a lot of compromise. She would have to be patient with him.

Honestly, what did it say about his childhood that he'd never considered sharing a living space with his own wife? A person didn't grow up like that without collecting scars along the way. She would have to be pretty coldhearted not to cut him some slack.

The more she thought about it over the course of the week, when she took the time to consider his feelings, more than being hurt, she felt sad. For him, because of the loving environment he deserved, and obviously never had. She would show him how unconditional love and dedication felt. No matter what it took.

Everything was going to work out all right.

She kept telling herself that all week as last-minute preparations were being made, and when her bridesmaids and mother arrived for the rehearsal luncheon Thursday afternoon.

She chanted it over and over during the final dress fittings, and later at the impromptu bridal dinner Sophie hosted at her residence. While everyone sipped champagne and shared stories of love and re-lationships, Hannah pasted on a smile to hide the fact that, for the first time since she made the decision to do this, she was questioning herself.

She even pretended, when her mother mentioned her own impending wedding, that she wasn't horri-fied by the idea. And when everyone gushed over the palace and asked her if royal life was everything she had dreamed of, she told them yes. Because it was, or, it *would* be. At least she hoped so.

It was after midnight when everyone retired to their rooms, and Hannah was finally alone, with nothing but time to think about what she was doing. It wasn't as if she could back out at this point. Not that she would even want to. She was just confused and scared.

What if she was making a mistake?

What she needed was a sign. She needed something to happen that would assure her she was doing the right thing.

She'd barely completed the thought when someone knocked on her door. Then she heard Phillip's voice.

"Hannah, it's me."

She rushed to the door before he could open it. As desperately as she wanted to see him, with the wedding less than twenty-four hours away, she couldn't. It would be bad luck and, honestly, she didn't need another black cloud hanging over her head.

She opened the door a crack, and stood behind it, so she wouldn't be tempted to look. "We can't see each other."

"I know," he said, his tone hushed. "I just wanted to let you know that I'm back from the States. I didn't want you to worry that I might be late for our wedding."

"How was your trip?"

"Exhausting. I toured ten resorts in five days. I'm glad to be home."

And she was glad he came home.

"I ran into Sophie downstairs. She said there was a bridal party tonight."

"It was fun," Hannah said. "It was nice to see all of my friends again. You'll meet them tomorrow."

"Sophie also said that she thought you might be upset about something."

How could Sophie have known? Hannah had been so careful not to let it show. "Why would she think that?"

"I don't know. But I wanted to make sure you're okay."

He was worried about her.

Though it was a small thing, for her, it meant so much. "I'm okay."

"I'm glad," he said. And she could hear that he was honestly relieved. "I worried you might be having second thoughts."

Was he seriously thinking that she wouldn't marry him? The idea that he could be even the slightest bit unsure made her feel a million times better. It made her realize that she wasn't in this alone. "Are you?"

There was a pause, then an emphatic, "No. I'm not."

She smiled. Neither was she any longer. "I'm not either."

"I missed you," he said. He sounded a little surprised. Like he hadn't expected to miss her, but it just…happened.

This was it. This was her sign.

"I missed you, too," she told him.

"I'm going to get to bed. I'll see you tomorrow. Sleep well."

"You, too."

She heard his footsteps as he walked away, then she closed the door and leaned against it.

The sense of dread she had been feeling all week was suddenly gone. The gush of relief that replaced it was so swift and intense her knees nearly buckled. Tomorrow she'd be Queen Hannah Augustus Mead.

Ten

The next day rushed by in a blur. Hannah was so busy, she barely had a moment to be nervous. And only when the time came to walk down the aisle, did she feel a twinge of sadness. Her father should have been here to give her away. But because there was no one in the world who could ever take his place, she insisted walking it alone.

When she saw Phillip standing at the end of the white runner, stoic and regal in his dress uniform, she felt a dizzying mix of excitement and nerves. And as she walked toward him and their eyes connected— when she saw a smile tug at the corners of his mouth and a dance in the depths of his eyes—a deep feeling of peace washed over her.

The ceremony itself was over quickly, and when the priest introduced them as husband and wife, the guests cheered.

Photographs seemed to take forever, and by the time they were escorted to the ballroom, the reception was already in full swing. Dinner was served shortly after, then they covered all of the formalities like the cutting of the cake and the first dance.

Her mother was her usual clingy self, and beginning to get on Hannah's nerves, until Sophie swooped in and whisked her away to meet some foreign dignitary.

As lovely as the party was, as much as she enjoyed seeing her friends and family, not to mention hobnobbing with the worlds elite, she couldn't seem to stop thinking about after the party. When she and Phillip would finally be alone, and free to do whatever they wanted.

She realized that Phillip was thinking the exact same thing when he stepped up beside her and asked, "How soon before we can leave?"

"At eleven o'clock we're to bid everyone farewell, so we can prepare to leave for our honeymoon." Even though there wasn't all that much preparing to do. Her maids had already packed her bags, and she was sure Phillip's had done the same.

She couldn't help but think that the instant they left, every single guest was going to know exactly what they were planning to do.

He pulled a pocket watch from his jacket and flipped it open. "It's ten-fifteen."

"So we should make the rounds one last time, say our goodbyes and thank-yous."

He took her arm. "That sounds like an excellent idea."

They went from group to group, thanking everyone for sharing their special day, hearing more congratulations and good wishes than she could count. There were even a few inquiries of how she felt now that she was officially queen.

"Honored," was her stock answer. Also terrified and unsure, but she didn't tell anyone that.

It was five minutes to eleven o'clock and they were saying good-night to the prime minister and his wife, when Hannah had a familiar and unsettling sensation she was being watched. She scanned the room briefly and when she reached the dessert table, her eyes caught on the source.

The dark-haired mystery woman.

She was staring intently at Hannah, this time with open hostility.

What could Hannah have done to a woman she had never even met, to earn such a look?

She wanted to point her out to Phillip, but he was in the middle of a conversation and she didn't want to appear rude by interrupting him. When she turned to look at the woman again, she was gone.

Hannah looked around frantically, trying to locate her, but it was as if she'd vanished. Like the last time, she even entertained the notion that she'd imagined her.

"Is something wrong?" Phillip asked.

She looked up to see that he was watching her with concern. She considered telling him about the woman, but what good would it do, now that she was gone? She smiled instead and said, "I'm fine. Just looking for my mother so I can say goodbye."

"Let's go find her so we can get out of here."

Hannah was sure the woman was no one, and she had nothing to be concerned about. So far her wedding day had been perfect, and she wasn't going to let anything ruin it.

Still, somewhere deep down, she couldn't help feeling the slightest twinge of something unpleasant. A foreshadow of something to come.

It was 11:15 p.m. by the time Phillip walked Hannah to her suite. He left to change out of his uniform while she went inside where her maids were waiting to help her out of her gown. To unfasten the row of miniscule buttons up the back.

It seemed to take forever, but finally she was free. She dismissed them immediately, so she'd have time to see to all the preparations she had been planning.

She took the box down from her closet, the one she had been saving for this day, and from inside of it pulled out the pure-white, silk-and-lace nightgown. She slipped it on and it dripped over her body like liquid, conforming to every curve.

Since Phillip liked her hair down, she fished out the pins then brushed out all the gel and hairspray until it lay shiny and soft against her shoulders. She dabbed a touch of perfume behind her ears and along her collarbone.

As Hannah asked, Elizabeth had decorated the bedroom with white candles. Dozens of them on every possible flat surface, all lit. When she turned out the lights, the effect was exactly what she had hoped for. Soft, flickering light.

The maids had turned the bed down and left two perfect red rosebuds, one on each pillow. A bottle of champagne chilled in a stand by the dresser.

It was exactly as she'd imagined.

"You've been busy," Phillip said.

She jolted with surprise and spun around. He stood, leaning in the bedroom doorway, watching her. He wore slacks and a long-sleeved silk shirt that was untucked and lay open. His skin looked warm and golden in the candlelight.

She felt absolutely naked in the scant gown, but she resisted the urge to cover herself. She didn't want him to know how nervous she was. "I didn't hear you knock."

"That's because I didn't. I thought you wouldn't mind, now that we're married." He walked toward her, a hungry look in his eyes as they raked over her. "It would seem that I'm overdressed."

The shirt slipped off his shoulders, down his arms and landed on the floor. The candles were supposed to make her look good, but, oh my goodness, he was beautiful.

He didn't stop until he was standing right in front of her. She just hoped he didn't notice the thud of her heart, the way her hands trembled. She didn't want him to know how nervous she felt.

He reached up and touched the lacey edge of the gown where it rested on the swell of her breast. "This is nice."

She swallowed hard, willing herself to relax.

"Nervous?" he asked.

"No," she said, but it came out as more of a squeak than an actual word. She cleared her throat and amended her answer to, "Maybe a little. Are you?"

He grinned and shook his head.

Of course he wasn't. Unlike her, he had done this before.

He leaned down, kissed her bare shoulder, his lips soft, his breath warm on her skin. "You smell good," he said.

So did he. She loved the way he smelled, the way he felt, yet she couldn't seem to make herself touch him.

Why was she so afraid? It wasn't as though she had never touched him before. But for some reason this time was different. Maybe because she knew what the end result would be.

His hands settled on her hips, large and steady, and she couldn't help it when she tensed.

"Relax, Hannah."

She took a deep breath and blew it out.

"I'm not sure what I'm supposed to do. This is my first time."

Rather than act disappointed, he smiled. Not condescending either. This was a smile of pure affection. "Just do what comes naturally. Act on your instincts."

That was the problem. Her instincts seemed to have lost their voice.

"You could start by touching me." He took her hand in his and pressed it flat against his chest. It felt so solid under her palm, his skin hot to the touch.

He tugged her closer, nuzzling the hollow behind her ear. It felt amazing, *better* than amazing.

He nipped the curve where her neck met her shoulder, making her skin shiver with awareness. "Honestly, I wasn't sure you were a virgin."

"You weren't?" How could he not tell?

"Not after that night in my suite. You seemed to have a pretty good grasp on what you were doing."

He kissed her throat, the line of her jaw. "This is no different."

His hands slid up her sides, his thumbs brushing the outermost edge of her breasts. She felt them tingle, the tips tighten into painful points.

"So, no man has touched you like this?" he asked.

"Nope."

"Never?"

She shook her head. She could see by his smile that he liked knowing she was his, and his only. She liked it, too.

"No one ever did this?" He cupped her breasts in his hands and a whimper slipped from her lips. His thumbs grazed back and forth, teasing her, and her skin went hot.

Then he picked her up and placed her on the bed. He unfastened his pants and slid them off.

Hannah couldn't help but be drawn to the front of his boxers. To the impressive-looking ridge underneath. She was no expert, but he looked...*generous*.

He settled beside her, propped up on his elbow,

smiling down at her. A sleepy, sexy grin. "Here we are."

"Here we are," she agreed. Finally. She had been beginning to feel as if this day would never come.

He brushed her breast with his lips. Once, then twice, then he took her in his mouth, silk and all, and the sensation was so shockingly intense that she gasped and arched her back.

She couldn't help wondering what other places he could use his mouth.

He hooked his index finger around one strap of her gown and eased it down her arm until her entire breast was exposed. And when he took her in his mouth this time, there was no fabric barrier. This time she felt *everything*. His tongue, his teeth. The wet heat.

A sound came out of her, like a moan, but more desperate, and she realized her fingers were tunneling through his hair. She was arching against his mouth, urging him to take more.

Phillip seemed to be fascinated by her. He kissed her breasts, her mouth, touched her in ways that made her shudder and quake. And her own hands seemed to have taken on a life of their own, exploring the secrets of his body, touching him like she had only imagined in her most intimate fantasies.

It wasn't long before the gown that was meant to arouse him was only getting in the way.

"This has to go," he ordered, helping her tug it up over her head, until the only thing left was a pair of scant thong panties made of the same fragile lace. Then he just looked at her, his eyes dark with arousal. "You're beautiful."

She felt beautiful, and not the least bit afraid. In fact, she couldn't imagine why she had been so nervous. This was so absolutely and completely right. She had never felt so close to him. To *anyone*.

He touched the minuscule triangle of lace between her thighs and it felt so amazing she nearly vaulted off the bed.

He eased her thong down her legs so slowly that she got impatient and kicked it the rest of the way off. Then she did something that surprised them both. She reached for the waistband of his boxers and tugged at them. She wanted them both to be naked.

He captured her mouth with his and kissed the last of her sense completely away. She didn't think she could be any more aroused, but somehow Phillip managed. Kissing her, touching her, until she could hardly stand it.

What felt like hours later, he eased himself over her, between her thighs. "I'll take it slow."

But she didn't want slow. She wanted to feel all of him now. She reached for his hips and pushed them hard against her.

She shuddered a moment, and then the pain was gone. What she felt instead was indescribable. She felt…complete. The ultimate in closeness.

He thrust into her, slowly at first, then faster.

She wound her legs around his, dug her nails into his shoulders. "Phillip," she begged, even though she had no idea what she was begging for.

He thrust himself inside her again, harder this time, and she was so stunned by the sensation she cried out.

He eased back and thrust again. Phillip could feel her inner walls flex and contract around him. Her eyes looked bleary and unfocused and her skin was blushed and hot.

He had never seen anything more arousing or sexy. Had never been with a woman so easy to please. And though it was taking every bit of concentration he could muster to maintain control, he didn't want to rush this.

But he could feel her losing it, feel her body clenching down on him. Then she tensed and bucked up against him. Her eyes went wide and sightless, with shock and pleasure and wonder. That was all it took. He lost it. His body coiled then released, letting go in a hot rush that seemed to wring the last trace of energy from his very cells. And for a minute, he couldn't find the strength to do more than breathe.

* * *

Hannah was gazing up at him, looking just as physically spent as he felt. Her cheeks and chest were deep red and her breath was coming in short, sharp bursts.

"Are you okay?"

She nodded, but when he shifted his weight, she grimaced.

"Hurt?"

"A little," she admitted.

He eased off her slowly, then he rolled onto his back and pulled her along with him. She curled up against his side in the crook of his arm, soft and warm and boneless, her head resting on his shoulder. The covers had somehow wound up in a bunch at their feet, but it didn't matter. He was so relaxed he felt as if he were melting into the mattress.

Oddly, it was perfect.

Getting married, saying the vows, hadn't been the disconcerting experience he had expected. When Sophie came to him the night before to say that Hannah was upset, the idea of her changing her mind, of her backing out and moving back to America, made him realize just how fond of her he'd become.

He just hoped that would be enough.

They were quiet for several minutes while their breathing evened out and pulses returned to normal.

"Is it always like that?" she asked.

"Like what?"

"It just felt so…so…*good.* I thought that wasn't supposed to happen. Not my first time."

He shrugged. "I guess you're a natural."

That made her smile. "Do we have to wait long?"

"For what?"

"To do it again?"

Already? "I thought you were sore."

"Not anymore." She put her hand on his stomach, a little shyly, but insatiably curious, and that was all it took for him.

He rolled her onto her back and smiled down at her. "Who says we have to wait?"

It was her innocence and her honesty, her complete trust, that was such a turn-on. But what did that mean for their future?

She would only be innocent for so long. Then what?

Eventually the novelty was going to wear off. It would become a duty instead of a pleasure, until the day came when they didn't bother at all.

She wrapped her arms around his neck and pulled him down for a kiss, and he decided not to worry about that now.

He would just enjoy it while it lasted.

Eleven

They left early the next morning for the private yacht off the coast of Monaco where they would be spending their honeymoon. In a way Phillip was dreading it. Two weeks, stuck in close quarters with the same woman. It was bound to get monotonous.

He spent most of the flight devising excuses to get them back to the palace early, and trying to determine how soon he could suggest going back without upsetting her too much. At least a week, he decided. By then he should be crawling out of his skin.

The first day, all they managed, on so little sleep, was to lie around and sun themselves, occasionally dipping in the water to cool off. They snacked on caviar and sipped champagne. And every so often Hannah would get this look, and next thing he knew, they would be tumbling into bed.

The second day was much of the same, and because it was rare that he allowed himself the privilege of just laying around and doing nothing, he let himself enjoy it.

Monday, Phillip and Hannah went ashore. They spent the day sightseeing and shopping, where he expected to put his credit card to good use, but Hannah surprised him again by showing little interest in spending his money. She only purchased a few modest souvenirs for family and friends, and she used her own money.

When he noticed her admiring a sapphire teardrop pendant necklace in a shop window, and saw the way her eyes lit, he suggested they go in and buy it.

She shook her head and said, "It's too much."

"You like it?"

She shrugged, but he could see that she was holding back.

"Do you *like* it?"

She bit her lip and nodded.

"Then let's get it." He took her hand and reached for the door handle but she resisted.

"I don't *need* it, Phillip."

"Consider it a wedding gift."

"But—"

"Let's at least look at it."

It took several more minutes of cajoling, and he still had to practically drag her into the shop. But when the salesclerk took the necklace from the case and handed it to Hannah, he knew he had her. With little argument, she allowed him to purchase it for her, and it surprised him how much her happiness pleased him.

Rather than let the bodyguard stow it with the rest of their packages, she insisted on wearing it. And as they walked, she kept one hand in his, and the other at her throat, smiling and fingering the gem as though it were the most precious thing she had ever owned. And she must have thanked him a dozen times.

"You act as if no one ever bought you a present," he said. "I thought your father was very wealthy."

"He was. But he also believed it was important to teach me the value of a dollar. I received gifts for the usual occasions. Holidays and birthdays and graduations. But nothing too extravagant. If I wanted something, I had to earn it."

"Like what, for example?"

"My first car. Daddy said owning a car is a privilege I had to earn. I worked in his office for a year before getting my license. Weekends during the school year so it wouldn't interrupt my studies, and five days a week during the summer. When I finally did get a car, all that hard work made me appreciate it. I took such good care of it that I drove it through the rest of high school and all through college."

"Even though you could have afforded a new car?"

She shrugged. "There was nothing wrong with the one I had."

Hannah never ceased to fascinate him. Just when he thought he had her figured out, she would do or say something to completely skew his impression of her.

"Does it bother you to always have someone watching you?" Hannah asked, referring to the bodyguards who shadowed their every step.

He shrugged. "It's always been that way."

"But don't you ever get tired of it? Do you ever wish you could be completely alone?"

"Sometimes, but I have a duty to my country to stay alive," he joked, and she laughed.

She seemed to find him genuinely entertaining, and he could recognize counterfeit laughter a mile away. He liked that he could make her happy so effortlessly. He'd dated women in the past who needed constant attention and ego stroking. He was beginning to believe that Hannah was one of the most low-maintenance women he'd ever known.

And what he liked even more was that she had a

mind of her own. He was accustomed to everyone doing exactly as he asked. Especially women. But Hannah wasn't afraid to question his motives. And often it took nothing more than a look. He might have suspected her to be manipulative, but he honestly didn't believe she had a deceitful bone in her body. She was too sweet and honest. Yet still managed to possess the resolve and character of ten men.

He liked her. Probably too much for either of their best interests.

Tuesday morning they docked in *Port De Font-vieille* where they would spend the day as guests of the Grimaldi family, with whom he'd been friends with since childhood. Yet, all he could think about over the course of the day was getting back to the ship so he and Hannah could be alone.

He'd never met a woman so curious or honest in bed. So responsive to his touch, or willing to experiment. And she was a quick study. Every day she became more and more adventurous.

Phillip kept waiting to get restless. For the familiar edgy feeling that would signal it was time to cut their vacation short and get back to the palace. He even had the perfect excuse. This was an arrangement. He was fulfilling his duty and shouldn't be having a problem controlling his urges. But, well into their second week, he began to realize that he wasn't growing restless. Spending time with her wasn't the burden he'd imagined. He liked her. She was witty and smart. And fun. He could talk to her. Intelligent conversations. He would even find himself telling her things that he'd never told anyone. Personal things. Even more odd, he felt as though he could trust her. Though it went against everything he had learned.

As the last day of their vacation drew closer, he found himself wishing it were longer. Which meant nothing, he told himself, other than the fact that she had preoccupied him longer than most. They would return to the palace, get back to *normal* life. He would go his way and she hers, meeting in the middle every so often. Often enough to placate her.

And as tempted as he might be to let things slide for just a while, he would be treading on dangerous ground. It was more important now than ever to draw the line. To make it clear exactly where she stood.

She wouldn't be happy about that. Not at first, but she would become used to the way things were. And maybe she wouldn't be happy, but she would adjust. She would adopt a cause, or find some purpose in her life that would keep her occupied. Then, when the children began to come along, she would immerse herself in being a mother.

And he was confident that she would be an exceptional one. Their children would know what it felt liked to be loved. And even if he wasn't capable, Hannah would love them enough for the both of them.

Though he couldn't help thinking that Hannah deserved so much better than that.

Twelve

They returned late Saturday night from their honeymoon to find that Hannah's new suite was finished and all of her things already moved in. But she was so exhausted, she didn't have the energy to investigate.

She stood in her sitting room Sunday morning, as her maids unpacked her things, taking in each and every detail. It was gorgeous, and exactly as she'd planned, but her excitement fell flat. As close as she and Phillip had become over their honeymoon, she half expected him to say he'd changed his mind, that he wanted to share a suite with her. When that didn't happen, when he chose to sleep in his own suite last

night—*alone*—she felt a deep sting of disappointment. Apparently things would go back to the way
they had been before the wedding.

But what had she expected? That in two weeks,
everything would change? That he would come home
a new man?

Okay, maybe she *had* expected it. Or, at the very
least, wished for it. But these things took time. It
would take a lot longer than fourteen days to over-
come years of abuse and dysfunction. Which is
exactly what Phillip had endured, though it had been
kept well hidden behind the royal crest. His parents'
treatment of him was reprehensible.

And a little voice in the back of her mind whispered, *Like father like son?* Would he do the same to
his children? But she would never let that happen. Her
and Phillip's children would know they were loved.

"Welcome home."

She sighed and turned to see Elizabeth standing
in the doorway.

Elizabeth smiled. "You asked me to remind you
about the gifts in the study."

Wedding gifts from all over the world had begun
arriving the Monday before the wedding. And since
her regular schedule didn't resume until tomorrow,
she figured it would be best to get everything taken
care of this afternoon. "Why don't we go take a look?"

They stepped out into the hall together and headed toward the stairs.

"Did you have a nice vacation?" Elizabeth asked. "I hear Monaco is lovely this time of year."

"The weather was perfect. We had a wonderful time together. How about you? Did you take any time off while I was gone?"

She was being nosy, but after learning Elizabeth didn't even have a boyfriend, Hannah insisted that she worked too hard. She was too young to be alone. She needed to live a little. But Hannah could see from her expression that Elizabeth hadn't taken her advice.

"I've been so busy with plans for the gala, I haven't really had time."

"Maybe I could help you," Hannah said. "I don't know a lot about planning parties, but I'd like to learn. Since this is my home now, I should get more involved."

"I would be honored." They reached the study door and Elizabeth asked ominously, "Are you ready?"

Ready? How bad could it be?

She opened the door, and when Hannah saw the state of the room, she gasped. Then she blinked several times, to be sure it wasn't an optical illusion. "Oh my God."

"Most of them came the past two weeks while you were gone."

What had started out as a few dozen gifts was now hundreds—heck, maybe even a *thousand*. Ornately wrapped packages in every conceivable size and shape were stacked nearly waist high in one corner of the study. "Who are they all from?"

"Government representatives, friends and relatives, business executives. They came in from all over the world."

No way she could open all these in one afternoon. It could take weeks to sort through it all, and she dreaded the nightmare of writing all the thank-you cards.

"It's something, isn't it?"

Hannah turned to find Sophie standing behind them. "I can't believe it. Is this normal?"

Sophie shrugged. "The last time anyone around here got married, it was my parents, and I wasn't around for that."

"It's going to take forever to open them all."

"Not if you have help," Sophie said. "I'm free today."

"Me, too," Elizabeth said. "I'm sure your maids would be happy to help as well. And we could probably round up a few other people."

"And what about Phillip?" Sophie asked.

Hannah could ask, or insist even, since they were his gifts as well as hers, but she had the very distinct feeling he needed some space. Though he never once, in the entire two weeks of their vacation, seemed restless or claustrophobic, the minute they returned home he immediately retreated to his suite. But not before mentioning a golf outing he had planned with his cousin today. Even though they were technically still on their honeymoon until tonight.

"He's spending the day with Charles," Hannah told her, and she could swear she saw disapproval in her sister-in-law's eyes. But for whom? Phillip for leaving, or Hannah for allowing it?

She wasn't sure she wanted to know. It disturbed her to think that Sophie might be disappointed in her, though she wasn't sure why. Maybe because Sophie was so strong. She seemed to know exactly what she wanted and wasn't afraid to fight for it.

Hannah hoped that someday she could be like that.

"The most efficient way to handle this would be two people per gift," Hannah reasoned. "One to open, the other to write down the sender and what the gift is."

"Sounds like a good idea," Sophie agreed. "Elizabeth, why don't you gather everything we need, and everyone you can find to help. I'll call over to the house and see what my housekeeper is up to."

"And I'll start sorting," Hannah said.

After Elizabeth left to round up more help, Sophie asked, "How was your honeymoon?"

"It was wonderful. Perfect."

"And now he's pulling a disappearing act?"

"It's not like that," Hannah told her, even though she suspected it was. "After two weeks solid together, who wouldn't need a break?"

"You, I suspect."

She hated that Sophie could read her so well.

"You didn't even sleep in the same room last night," Sophie added.

How could she possibly know that? "What, do you have spies in the palace watching us?"

"Who needs spies? Your rooms face my residence and I know every window in this place. The lights were on in both your suites last night."

Hannah didn't know what to say, what she *could* say, to convince Sophie that everything was okay. So she didn't even try. "It's just going to take time."

"You really believe that?"

"Yes, as a matter of fact I do. I'm committed to make this work."

Sophie smiled. "You'll be okay, then."

Hannah must have looked confused, because Sophie chuckled. "I like you, Hannah. I think you're good for my brother. He needs someone to give him a swift kick in the ass every now and then. Remind him that he's worthy."

"Worthy?"

"Of love. Of happiness."

"Why would he think that? I know your parents were cold, but that certainly wasn't any fault of yours and Phillip's."

"Try telling that to a young child. When your parents don't show you love and affection, you feel as if there's something wrong with you. You think that, for whatever reason, you're not lovable."

Hannah couldn't even imagine how that would feel. The idea of her parents not loving her was so far out of her range of comprehension.

"Add to that all of the women showering him with false affection. For the money, or the crown, or whatever their particular agenda might be. You never know who to trust."

"You seem to get it."

"*Getting it* doesn't mean anything. I've never been in a relationship that lasted more than four months, Hannah. Why do you think that is?" She shrugged. "It's like telling an alcoholic they have to stop drinking and expecting them to go cold turkey."

That was just so...*sad.*

Sophie must have read her expression. "I'm not telling you this so you'll feel sorry for me. I just want you to know what you're up against. He really cares for you. I can tell. Even if he's not so great at showing it. It's going to take time."

"I'm not in a rush. I'm determined to make this work. No matter what or how long it takes."

Sophie smiled. "I'm glad. Now, enough of this. I'm going to call home and see if I can wrangle up a bit more help."

"I'll start sorting this mess."

"Back in a few," Sophie said, then she was gone.

Until just then, Hannah hadn't realized how lucky she was, how good her parents had been to her. And she felt bad for the way she'd been treating her mother.

Her mother was right when she said Hannah wasn't being fair. Maybe she just didn't like that she wasn't the center of her mother's world any longer. She was in limbo. Not a part of her old life any longer, but not quite into her new one yet.

She felt unsure of what she was supposed to be. In the past she would go to her father for advice, to help her sort things through, since he knew her better than anyone in the world. He understood her.

With him gone, for the first time in her life, she was entirely on her own.

It was past 10:00 p.m. when Phillip returned to the palace. He noticed the light on in the study and walked over to investigate. There he found Hannah, sitting on the floor, opening wedding gifts.

He realized he was happy to see her. He'd thought of little else all day but her smile. Which is why he'd made it a point to stay away. He didn't want her getting the wrong idea. He didn't want to delude her into believing that anything had changed.

The mountain of packages that had been there last night when he stepped in to get a book had been reduced by at least half. What was left of the wrapped gifts was on one side of the room, sorted by size, and the opened ones still in boxes on the opposite side.

"Did you do all this on your own?" he asked.

She looked up at him, but her smile wasn't as bright as usual. "I had help. I hope you don't mind that we started without you."

He stepped farther into the room. "I don't mind."

"That's what I figured."

She was still wearing the necklace he gave her. As far as he knew, she hadn't taken it off yet. "Did we get anything good?"

"Lots of crystal and silver. Kitchen and bed linen. I can't begin to imagine where we'll put it all."

"Storage?" he suggested.

"But doesn't that seem like a waste? I'm flattered by everyone's generosity, but I can't help feeling that it's too much."

She looked genuinely distressed, and it occurred to him that her chilly greeting had nothing to do with his behavior. She was upset over the gifts. It was her conscience distressing her, not his apparent relationship phobia. And despite telling himself otherwise, he was relieved. Seeing her unhappy was unpleasant enough. Knowing it was his fault made him feel unfit.

He was royalty, the leader of his country, yet somehow she managed to make him feel…inferior. And she did it without even trying, because Hannah wouldn't have the first clue how to be vindictive. The word wasn't even in her vocabulary.

He sat down beside her on the floor and she leaned against him, letting her head drop against his shoulder.

"It feels wrong that we've received all these lavish and, to be honest, *excessive* gifts when so many people around the world lack the basic necessities."

"So what do you want to do?"

"I did have an idea. Maybe we could sponsor an auction and the proceeds could be donated to charity."

"Auction off our wedding gifts? You don't think people would be offended?"

"We can release a statement. Something about how grateful we are, but we want to share it with the rest of the world. I'm sure your press people can put just the right spin on it."

If so, it would make the royal family look good,

not that he suspected for a second that image was her concern. She was just a generous, caring person.

"Because there's so much," she said, "we would probably have to do a live auction for the more valuable pieces and a silent auction for the smaller stuff."

He looked down at her and smiled. "I think it's an excellent idea."

Her face lit up. "Really?"

"I do. First thing tomorrow, I'll look into it."

"Thank you!" She threw her arms around his neck and hugged him, and he scooped her up and sat her in his lap.

Ah, yes. This was what he needed, what he had been craving since last night when he went to bed alone. Not that he'd slept much. In two weeks' time, sleeping alone had lost its appeal. But like everything else, eventually the novelty would wear off.

"Why don't we go to bed?" he suggested.

"We, as in, both of us together? In the same bed?"

"That was the idea." Although, after last night, he couldn't really blame her for being unsure. "If that's okay with you."

She smiled, happy once again. "Your bed or mine?"

"Yours."

"I need to take a shower first."

He rose to his feet and pulled her along with him. "Perhaps I should join you."

She gave him that wicked smile. "You know I love you all soapy and slippery."

And that feeling, he decided, was most definitely mutual.

Thirteen

The weeks that followed their honeymoon flew by for Hannah. Between organizing the auction, which would take place just before the holiday season, and planning the gala, which would happen in the spring—not to mention her regular royal duties and cooking lessons with Sophie—she barely had a free moment.

Phillip's schedule was no less hectic. Though they didn't always manage dinner together, their nights—when he wasn't traveling—were reserved for each other. They alternated between his and her suite. They made love often, although there were times when they were both too exhausted to do more than lie in bed and watch the evening news, fighting to keep their eyes open.

Somehow, since she had moved to Morgan Isle, she and Phillip had become a couple. And while it wasn't exactly the way she had planned on and dreamed about, different was all right. It kept things interesting. It was more work than she had imagined, but she was happy, and Phillip was, too.

At least, that was what she thought.

The afternoon of the auction, she was a nervous wreck, hoping everything went well. What if no one showed? What if people really were insulted that she and Phillip would cast off their gifts?

"You're worrying for nothing," Phillip assured her. "It's going to be a huge success."

And as with most situations like this, he was right. The moment the doors opened, the room flooded with people. Two hours later, just before the bidding for the live auction was to begin, it was standing room only.

She and Phillip were making the rounds, socializing and drumming up business, when she felt that disturbing, familiar sensation of being watched. Sure enough, when she scanned the room, her eyes connected with those of the mystery woman.

She nudged Phillip to get his attention. When he saw her face, he frowned. "What's the matter?"

"That woman is here."

"What woman?"

"The one who was staring at me the afternoon I arrived. I saw her at our wedding, too."

"Where?" he asked.

She gestured in her general direction. "Long dark hair. Really attractive."

She could tell the instant Phillip saw her, the way recognition lit his eyes, that he knew her. And rather than look away, the woman smiled and waved to him. Then she started walking toward them and Hannah's heart bottomed out.

Finally, she would meet face-to-face with the woman who so openly resented her. Though she was relieved to be getting it over with, her hands still trembled. She was so beautiful, and she practically oozed sensuality. In contrast, Hannah looked almost plain and dowdy.

"Phillip!" she said, her voice low and sultry. "So good to see you again!"

Phillip didn't look as if he shared the sentiment, but he was polite. "Madeline, hello."

She accepted his outstretched hand, then took it a step further by kissing his cheek. No one would be so bold, unless they had a somewhat intimate relationship with the king. And it was more than obvious these two did. And to do it right in front of Hannah? No doubt this woman had some kind of agenda.

"Hannah, this is Madeline Grenaugh," Phillip said. "Madeline, this is my wife."

"Your Highness," she said, but the words dripped with barely masked distaste, then she dipped into the most pathetic excuse for a curtsy Hannah had ever seen. The tension was so thick it seemed to cling to her skin and clothes, fill the chambers of her lungs until it was difficult to breathe.

"Well, the auction will be starting soon," Phillip said, and Hannah could see that he was antsy to move on.

"Yes, I should decide which pieces I plan to bid on. It was a pleasure to finally meet you, Hannah."

Not addressing Hannah by her title was a direct and blatant insult, nor did she bother to curtsy. Phillip didn't seem to notice, or didn't care.

"I'll see you again very soon," she told Phillip, and gave him a smile, as though they shared some sort of secret. And as she walked away, she leaned close to Hannah and said under her breath, "You may be his wife, but I'll always be the one he loves."

Hannah was so stunned she didn't know what to say. She stood there frozen, dumbfounded.

"What did she say to you?" Phillip asked.

Hannah shook her head. Phillip looked as though he might push the issue, but then someone else approached them and he seemed to forget about it altogether.

Hannah couldn't though.

She wasn't foolish enough to believe that Phillip had no women in his life before her, but to have one thrown in her face was more disturbing than she could have dreamed. Especially one who looked like that. And what if Madeline had been telling the truth? What if Phillip *did* love her?

No, that was ridiculous.

Phillip loved Hannah. He may not have been able to say the words, but he expressed his feelings in so many different ways. She could even live her entire life without actually hearing him say the words, just as long as his actions spoke for him.

Couldn't she?

By the time they got home late that evening, Hannah felt as if she'd been in a knock-down, drag-out fight with every one of her fears and insecurities. And she was losing.

She followed Phillip to his suite, sat on the edge of the bed while he undressed.

"Long night," he said.

"Yes, it was," she agreed.

He unlooped his tie, slipped it off and draped it over the chair by the closet. "I'm exhausted."

"Me, too."

He shrugged out of his jacket, and tossed it on top

of the tie, then he turned to her, unsnapping his cuff links. "So, are you going to tell me?"

"Tell you what?"

He dropped his cuff links on the bureau. "What's wrong."

For a second she considered denying it was anything other than fatigue. But it had been nagging her all night and she couldn't hold it in any longer. "Madeline Grenaugh."

"What about her?"

"Who is she?"

"She's a family friend."

"I get the feeling she was a lot more than a friend."

He sighed, looking resigned, as if he'd been expecting this. "What did she say to you?"

"She insinuated that you and she had a relationship."

"We saw each other on and off for a while, yes."

"Was it serious?"

"She seemed to think so. She had herself convinced we would get married, even though I never said a word to give her that impression. When the engagement was announced, she was quite…upset."

"Did you sleep with her?" The question was out before she even realized she wanted to ask it.

"Don't do this, Hannah."

"I want to know."

"Do you really?"

She could tell by his reaction that the answer was yes. She knew she was being unreasonable, but for reasons that made no sense to her, she needed to hear it from him. She needed to hear him say the words. "Did you sleep with her, Phillip?"

He paused, searching her face. At least he had the guts to meet her eye. Finally, he said, "Yes. I did."

She knew it, but it still hurt.

"It was a long time ago, and I refuse to apologize for something I did before we were married."

Nor should he have to. "Are you in love with her?"

He cursed under his breath. "No, Hannah. I am not now, nor was I *ever* in love with her. Or anyone else for that matter."

"Including me. Is that what you mean?"

He only stared at her.

And then she couldn't hold back any longer. "I love you, Phillip."

His expression didn't change, didn't soften with affection. He didn't look sad, or regretful. Just…cold. "Your love is wasted on me."

That stung more than she could have imagined. To offer him her love and have it thrown back in her face. "How can you say that?"

"Because I can't love you back. I'm not capable."

"You have feelings for me, Phillip. I *know* you do.

You've shown it in a million little ways. Why can't you just trust them?"

He shook his head. "I knew this was a bad idea."

"What?"

"This." He gestured to the bed, around the room. "Us being in such close quarters. I've given you the wrong idea, led you to think this is something it isn't."

"What *isn't* it?"

"A marriage. Not the kind you expect. I've already told you this."

But it was. Why couldn't he see that? "So why did you?"

He didn't seem to know how to answer that, but finally he said, "It's important we give the impression that we have a good marriage."

"And here I thought it would be more important that we actually *have* a good marriage. Not to mention that what we do in private has nothing to do with public image."

"And that's my fault. I'm sorry. But I told you how this was going to be."

"You're *sorry?*" She wanted to grab him by the front of his shirt and shake some sense into him, convince him that it was okay to feel. To love her.

"I will never be unfaithful to you, Hannah."

"Wow, *thanks*."

Her sarcasm seemed to surprise him. And she

couldn't resist twisting the knife. "Although, honestly, I can't see the point in either of us remaining faithful in a marriage that isn't real."

His expression darkened. "What is that supposed to mean?"

She could see he was interpreting her words to mean that she wouldn't be faithful. As he should. But she couldn't imagine, if he had no feelings for her, why he would care.

"Nothing, Phillip. It doesn't mean anything." She got up and grabbed her purse.

"Where are you going?"

"To bed. You know, you have your suite, I have mine."

Phillip's mouth pulled into a stubborn, straight line. He nodded. "Fine."

All he had to do was ask her to stay, and she probably would, but he couldn't even manage that. And she could only assume it was because he didn't care. And she was too angry to stay and try to talk some sense into him. She would only wind up saying something she regretted.

She stopped at the door and turned to him. "Out of curiosity, what about children?"

"What about them?"

"You say you're not capable of love. Does that apply to your children, too?"

She could swear he paled a shade. And for the first time since she had known him, he looked genuinely uneasy. Finally, he said, "You'll love them enough for the both of us."

"You know, I feel sorry for you, Phillip. You'll be miserable your whole life." She turned and left him there, drained and disappointed. And deep down she knew it was the beginning of the end.

"How does roast duck sound?" Sophie asked Hannah.

They sat together in Hannah's suite, discussing the menu for the gala.

Hannah shrugged. She honestly couldn't care less. She didn't care about much of anything these days. She and Phillip barely spoke more than a word or two in the weeks following the auction. And Hannah had never felt so isolated or lonely in her life. On top of that, she'd been feeling under the weather for the last few days. If it weren't for Sophie and the friendship they had formed, Hannah might not have been able to stand it.

They spent many evenings together, the time Hannah used to spend with her husband. They had even begun the cooking lessons Sophie had promised, but Hannah had given up after the first few. Every time she even looked at food she felt sick to her stomach.

In fact, she felt sick almost all the time. Sick in her heart and in her soul. She knew what she had to do, she just hadn't managed to work up the courage yet.

She kept telling herself that maybe he would come around. And every day that he didn't, she could feel her hope deflating. She thought she could do this. She thought she could make this work, but she just wasn't strong enough.

"I have a new recipe I wanted to try," Sophie said. "I was hoping you and Phillip would be my guinea pigs. How about dinner, Friday, at my place?"

Why? So she and Phillip could go through the motions? Pretend that everything was okay? That she wasn't miserable?

She knew Sophie was trying to help, but Hannah was past believing there *was* hope for them.

"Hannah?"

"I don't think…" Her voice broke.

"I know you guys have been going through a rough patch."

"Rough patch?" Tears welled up in her eyes.

Sophie touched her arm, her eyes so full of sympathy, Hannah could barely stand it. She tried to swallow the tears down, but it was no use. They spilled over onto her cheeks.

She swiped at her face with the corner of her

sleeve, embarrassed and disgusted with herself for being so weak. "What the heck is wrong with me?"

"You're upset. It's understandable."

"But I'm not like this. I can't seem to stop crying."

"PMS?" Sophie suggested.

"Maybe." It was as good an excuse as any.

She handed Hannah a tissue. "When is your period due?"

Hannah shrugged and dabbed away the tears. "Probably soon. I haven't really been keeping track."

"How long has it been?"

"I'm not sure. Why?"

"Is it possible you could be late?"

"*Late?* No, of course not." Surely it couldn't have been that long.

"Maybe you should check. Just in case."

It was a waste of time, but to appease Sophie, she crossed the room to her desk and rifled around the top drawer for her personal planner. Flipping through, she was stunned to see that the last red check, indicating the first day of her cycle, was nearly five weeks ago.

Her heart sank. Had it really been that long?

No, that couldn't be right. It had to be a mistake.

"Well?" Sophie asked.

"According to this, I should have started a week ago," she told her, feeling a wave of nausea so intense she nearly gagged. "You don't think…"

"Have you been taking precautions?"

"No, but…it's only been a few months. It took my parents years to get pregnant. I just assumed…"

"It only takes one time, on just the right day."

Well, in that case, they certainly had their bases covered. Up until a couple of weeks ago, there hadn't been very many days when they *didn't* make love. "Do you really think…?"

Sophie took her hand and squeezed it. "What I think, is that we need to go see the family doctor."

Hannah sat on pins and needles, convincing herself it had to be a mistake—a glitch in her cycle from all the stress lately, despite the fact she'd always been regular as clockwork. Not to mention that she'd been feeling physically ill for two weeks now, but that could be easily explained. A touch of the flu, or even depression.

"You are not pregnant," she told herself, and had repeated the phrase at least a hundred times when the doctor came in to see her. He handed her a pregnancy test and showed her to the bathroom.

"I'll be right here if you need me," Sophie said.

Hannah had never so much as held a pregnancy test, much less had to use one. She flipped it over to read the directions.

It seemed odd that such a life-altering result could

come from such a simple procedure. Although, the result was going to be the same, no matter how long she waited. Negative. In fact, she would probably go in the bathroom to find that her period had already started. And miraculously without any of the cramping or bloating that typically preceded it.

It was as easy and quick as the box boasted. And when the result formed in the indicator window, she felt numb.

She opened the bathroom door. Sophie stood there waiting anxiously. "Well?"

"I'm not pregnant," Hannah said, then dissolved into tears.

Fourteen

After dismissing the physician, Sophie took Hannah in her arms and hugged her. "Don't be unhappy. It'll happen."

She wasn't unhappy. It was worse than that. She was *relieved*. And, at the same time, she was completely and utterly sad. Because she knew that this meant her marriage was over.

"He doesn't love me. He says he's not capable."

Sophie held her at arm's length. "Hannah—"

"And when I asked him about our children, if he could love them, he said I would love them enough for the both of us."

"He didn't mean it."

"Yes, he did. And I won't do that to a child."

"What are you saying?"

"I'm saying that I made a mistake, and maybe it's a mistake I need to fix."

Sophie clutched her hands. "Just give him time."

"How much time? Months? Years? I've wasted eight years already, grooming myself to be the perfect royal wife. What has he done for me, Sophie?"

She didn't seem to know how to answer that.

"I can't do this anymore. I *won't*." She wouldn't waste another minute on him.

"Please, Hannah, give him a chance to make things right."

"He's had chances." She shook her head, determined now. "Life is too short, and I deserve better. I've stayed too long already. I'm through compromising."

Sophie seemed to recognize that it was a losing battle, and Hannah wasn't going to budge. "What will you do?"

She had been thinking about that a lot lately. What she would do if she ever worked up the courage to leave him. "Go back home, to Seattle."

"And you really think he's just going to let you go?"

"He doesn't have a choice. This is still a free country. He doesn't own me."

Sophie didn't say anything, but Hannah could see that she was upset.

Then tears filled her eyes. Tough Sophie, who Hannah suspected didn't even possess tear ducts. "But I don't want you to go."

She hugged Sophie, and they cried together. Even though they wouldn't technically be sisters after she left Phillip, they could still be good friends.

Sophie barged into Phillip's office without knocking. "You're an idiot!"

He sighed and put down his pen. He tried to work up the will to be annoyed, but he couldn't manage it. It's not as if he'd been doing anything important. Just staring blindly at the document he was supposed to be reading.

Besides, Sophie had been giving him the silent treatment lately, and he was surprised to find he actually missed her. Although he had no doubt the tirade that was surely to follow had more to do with his marriage.

"Lovely to see you, too," he said.

"You're going to lose her. You realize that, right?"

Of course he did. In fact, he was counting on it. "It's for the best."

She looked absolutely appalled. "Are you kidding me? She's the best thing that ever happened to you.

Up until a couple of weeks ago, I've never seen you so happy."

His happiness wasn't the issue. "I can't give her what she needs."

"She's not asking for much. Just for you to let down the wall. She just wants you to love her. Which I suspect you already do. You're just too afraid, or too bloody stubborn to admit it."

"You couldn't possibly understand."

"Look who you're talking to, Phillip. They were my parents, too."

"It has nothing to do with them."

"It has *everything* to do with them. They did a lousy job raising us. But how much longer are we going to let it ruin our lives? Why can't we let ourselves be happy?"

They were who they were and nothing was going to change that. "It's over, Sophie."

"Talk to her, Phillip."

"There's nothing left to say."

For a moment she just stared, then she shook her head. "You're a coward." She stormed out, slamming the door behind her.

Maybe she was right. But since Hannah arrived, she had managed, single-handedly, to turn his entire life upside down.

He just wanted things back to the way they used

to be. And he hated to admit that the days of not communicating with her made him feel empty.

Hannah was unhappy and he had no one to blame but himself. How could he have been so careless, let this spin so far out of control?

He didn't want to hurt Hannah. He wished he could be everything she wanted and needed him to be, but he couldn't change who he was.

She had every right to be angry with him. And she deserved so much more than he was capable of giving. She deserved to be happy, to be with a man who could return all the love she had to offer. One who appreciated her in a way Phillip never could.

And he needed to find someone who would accept him for his limitations. One who was more concerned with the title than building a long-lasting love affair. Who would be content to raise his children, living a lavish lifestyle. That, at least, he could provide with a clear conscience.

Maybe it was time to face the truth. That this marriage didn't stand a chance.

But he realized that he wanted this marriage to work. He wanted Hannah in his life. But could he do that? Did he even know how?

He got up and walked to his bedroom, needing space to think.

He switched on the bedroom light, and something

on the covers caught his eye. He walked over to the bed and saw that it was the sapphire necklace he bought Hannah on their honeymoon.

At first he thought maybe she had dropped it there by accident the last time she was in his room, but that had been weeks ago. Besides, Phillip had seen it around her neck since then.

No, she put it here.

He might have thought it was her way of hurting him, rubbing it in. But that wasn't Hannah's style. If she was giving it back, there was a reason.

He thought about Sophie, the urgency in her pleas when she insisted he talk to Hannah, and his heart actually sank. He hated to admit it, but Sophie was right. He did love Hannah. He was not too scared and stubborn to admit it. He knew what he had to do now. He needed to get his wife back. He grabbed the necklace and walked to Hannah's suite.

Phillip found Hannah in the bedroom with several open, half-filled suitcases on the bed.

"What's going on here?" he said, but it came out harsher than he'd intended. More like a bark than a question.

If she noticed, she didn't let it show. She didn't even look up from the pile of clothes she was folding. "What does it look like?"

It looked like she was leaving, but for some reason he couldn't make himself say that.

This was what he wanted at first. But now it just felt so wrong.

"I figure, if I leave now, I can spend the holidays with my mother and be there for her wedding."

So she was just going home for the holidays? Then she would be back? He wished that were true, but he was sure that was merely wishful thinking.

He held up the necklace. "I found this in my room."

She finally looked up at him, her face tired and sad. "It didn't seem right, me keeping it."

"It was a gift. It's yours." He held it out. "Take it."

She took a deep, unsteady breath. "I can't. I'm sorry."

His hand fell to his side. "I'll hold it for you, until you come back."

"I'm not coming back."

The finality of her words jabbed him like a spear, directly through his heart.

"We can do this as quietly as possible," she said, folding as she talked. Probably so she didn't have to look at him. "I know there will be a certain amount of scandal, but I'll do what I can to keep it out of the press. I'll fade out of sight for a while. Until things settle down. And you can blame it on me. Say I was at fault."

She had it all figured out. And after everything,

she seemed to be more worried how her leaving would impact the royal family, than how it would affect her own life.

He wished she would stop being so bloody reasonable. Why didn't she fight this? Fight him?

"You're talking about a divorce."

"I can't do this anymore. I thought I was strong enough…." She shrugged. "I guess I was wrong."

Not strong enough? She was the strongest person he had ever known. Yet somehow he had managed to break her. He always told himself they would both be better off if she left; only now did he realize that he never really thought she would do it. And there was this feeling in his chest. This…*pain*. An ache in his heart like nothing he had ever felt before.

"Hannah…"

"Staying together would be unfair to both of us. I deserve to be with a man who loves me as much as I love him. And you deserve to have a wife who is willing to love you just the way you are."

So, by loving him, she felt she had wronged him somehow? That didn't even make sense. He was the one in the wrong here. He was the one with the problem, not her. She had done everything right.

Sophie was right. The last few months had been the happiest in his life. And the thought of his life without her in it, well, what was the point?

He closed the door, as if that alone could stop her. "You're not leaving."

"You just don't like the idea of losing."

"This has nothing to do with winning or losing. I don't want you to go."

"Why?"

"I don't want you to go because…" He struggled with the words, the right thing to say to make her understand, but all he could come up with was, "Because…*I love you.*"

They may have been the toughest three words he had ever said in his life, but the instant they were out, he knew they were true. He knew it with a certainty he'd never felt before. And he said it again, just to be sure he could. "I love you."

"These last few weeks I've been convincing myself that there was someone out there who would love you and make you happy. But I realized that I'm that someone. I've been fighting it for so long and I let my ideas of what a marriage was get in the way of my feelings for you."

Instead of looking elated, or throwing herself into his arms, Hannah just looked sad.

He took another step toward her, and when she didn't retreat, he took another, until she was close enough to touch. "Sophie was right. I am an idiot."

"You really want me to stay?"

"I don't just want you to stay. I *need* you, Hannah."

Tears welled up in her eyes, and she looked as though maybe she was starting to believe him. "You do?"

He nodded, feeling a little choked up himself. "Am I too late?"

"No." The tears spilled over onto her cheeks. "You're not too late."

He pulled her into his arms and held her tight, buried his nose in her hair. And she clung to him. It felt so good, so right that it stung. But it was the good kind of pain. And he swore that as long as he lived, he would never let go of her again.

She looked up at him, smiling through her tears. "You love me?"

He cupped her cheek, kissed her softly. "I love you."

Hannah buried her face against his chest and squeezed him so hard he could barely draw a breath. "Is this real, or am I dreaming?"

"It's real." In fact, he'd never felt anything so real in all his life. And now that he'd let himself feel, he couldn't seem to make it stop. He didn't want to. And to think that he'd almost let her go. He would live with that regret for the rest of his life.

"I'm so sorry, Hannah. I just didn't realize…I couldn't see it."

"Don't be sorry. You thought you were doing the

right thing. And like my dad used to say, nothing bad can come from telling the truth."

"But it wasn't the truth."

She shrugged. "But you didn't know that at the time. Besides, think how much more we'll appreciate each other. How much better it will be."

"I can't imagine that it gets much better than this."

She had that look, like she knew something he didn't. "It could."

"How?"

She took his hand and pressed it to her stomach, looked up at him and smiled. "We could have a baby."

"Right away."

She nodded. "I thought I might be, and when the test came back negative it made me realize how much I want children. I want us to have a baby, Phillip."

"I think that's a great idea. Maybe a little girl, just like you."

She smiled. "Or a little boy, just like his father."

If he was the type of man that cried, he would have lost it just then. As it was, he was having a hell of a time processing the overwhelming feelings of happiness.

"Think you can love us both?" she asked.

So he gave the honest answer. The only answer he could. "I already do."

* * * * *

The editors at Harlequin Blaze have never
been afraid to push the limits—
tempting readers with the forbidden,
whetting their appetites with a
wide variety of story lines.
But now we're breaking the final barrier—
the time barrier.

In July, watch for
BOUND TO PLEASE
By fan favorite Hope Tarr
Harlequin Blaze's first-ever
historical romance—a story that's
truly Blaze-worthy in every sense

Here's a sneak peek...

Brianna stretched out beside Ewan, languid as a cat, and promptly fell asleep. Midday sunshine streamed into the chamber, bathing her lovely, long-limbed body in golden light, the sea-scented breeze wafting inside to dry the damp red-gold tendrils curling about her flushed face. Propping himself up on one elbow, Ewan slid his gaze over her. She looked beautiful and whole, satisfied and sated, and altogether happier than he had so far seen her. A slight smile curved her beautiful lips as though she must be in the midst of a lovely dream. She'd molded her lush, lovely body to his and laid her head in the curve of his shoulder and settled in to sleep beside him. For the longest while he lay there turned toward her, content to watch her sleep, at near-perfect peace.

Not wholly perfect, for she had yet to answer his

marriage proposal. Still, she wanted to make a baby with him, and Ewan no longer viewed her plan as the travesty he once had. He wanted children—sons to carry on after him, though a bonny little daughter with flame-colored hair would be nice, too. But he also wanted more than to simply plant his seed and be on his way. He wanted to lie beside Brianna night upon night as she increased, rub soothing unguents into the swell of her belly, knead the ache from her back and make slow, gentle love to her. He wanted to hold his newly born child in his arms and look down into Brianna's tired but radiant face and blot the perspiration from her brow and be a husband to her in every way.

He gave her a gentle nudge. "Brie?"

"Hmmm?"

She rolled onto her side and he captured her against his chest. One arm wrapped about her waist, he bent to her ear and asked, "Do you think we might have just made a baby?"

Her eyes remained closed, but he felt her tense against him. "I don't know. We'll have to wait and see."

He stroked his hand over the flat plane of her belly. "You're so small and tight it's hard to imagine you increasing."

"All women increase no matter how large or small

they start out. I may not grow big as a croft, but I'll be big enough, though I have hopes I may not waddle like a duck, at least not too badly."

The reference to his fair-day teasing was not lost on him. He grinned. "Brianna MacLeod grown so large she must sit still for once in her life. I'll need the proof of my own eyes to believe it."

Despite their banter, he felt his spirits dip. Assuming they were so blessed, he wouldn't have the chance to see her thus. By then he would be long gone, restored to his clan according to the sad bargain they'd struck. He opened his mouth to ask her to marry him again and then clamped it closed, not wanting to spoil the moment, but the unspoken words weighed like a millstone on his heart.

The damnable bargain they'd struck was proving to be a devil's pact indeed.

* * * * *

Will these two star-crossed lovers
find their sexily-ever-after?
Find out in

BOUND TO PLEASE
By Hope Tarr
Available in July

Wherever Harlequin® Blaze™ books are sold

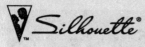

Silhouette®

Romantic
SUSPENSE

**Sparked by Danger,
Fueled by Passion.**

Conard County: The Next Generation

When he learns the truth about his father, military
man Ethan Parish is determined to reunite with his
long-lost family in Wyoming. On his way into town,
he clashes with policewoman Connie Halloran,
whose captivating beauty entices him. When
Connie's daughter is threatened, Ethan must use
his military skills to keep her safe. Together they
race against time to find the little girl and confront
the dangers inherent in family secrets.

Look for

A Soldier's Homecoming

by *New York Times*
bestselling author
Rachel Lee

Available in July wherever you buy books.

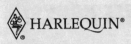

REQUEST YOUR FREE BOOKS!

2 FREE NOVELS PLUS 2 FREE GIFTS!

Passionate, Powerful, Provocative!

YES! Please send me 2 FREE Silhouette Desire® novels and my 2 FREE gifts (gifts are worth about $10). After receiving them, if I don't wish to receive any more books, I can return the shipping statement marked "cancel". If I don't cancel, I will receive 6 brand-new novels every month and be billed just $4.05 per book in the U.S. or $4.74 per book in Canada, plus 25¢ shipping and handling per book and applicable taxes, if any*. That's a savings of almost 15% off the cover price! I understand that accepting the 2 free books and gifts places me under no obligation to buy anything. I can always return a shipment and cancel at any time. Even if I never buy another book, the two free books and gifts are mine to keep forever.   225 SDN ERVX 326 SDN ERVM

Name _____ (PLEASE PRINT) _____

Address _____ Apt. # _____

City _____ State/Prov. _____ Zip/Postal Code _____

Signature (if under 18, a parent or guardian must sign) _____

Mail to the Silhouette Reader Service:
IN U.S.A.: P.O. Box 1867, Buffalo, NY 14240-1867
IN CANADA: P.O. Box 609, Fort Erie, Ontario L2A 5X3

Not valid to current subscribers of Silhouette Desire books.

Want to try two free books from another line?
Call 1-800-873-8635 or visit www.morefreebooks.com.

* Terms and prices subject to change without notice. N.Y. residents add applicable sales tax. Canadian residents will be charged applicable provincial taxes and GST. Offer not valid in Quebec. This offer is limited to one order per household. All orders subject to approval. Credit or debit balances in a customer's account(s) may be offset by any other outstanding balance owed by or to the customer. Please allow 4 to 6 weeks for delivery. Offer available while quantities last.

Your Privacy: Silhouette Books is committed to protecting your privacy. Our Privacy Policy is available online at www.eHarlequin.com or upon request from the Reader Service. From time to time we make our lists of customers available to reputable third parties who may have a product or service of interest to you. If you would prefer we not share your name and address, please check here. ☐

SDES08R

HIGH-SOCIETY SECRET PREGNANCY

Park Avenue Scandals

Self-made millionaire Max Rolland had given
up on love until he meets socialite fundraiser
Julia Prentice. After their encounter Julia finds
herself pregnant, but a mysterious blackmailer
threatens to use this surprise pregnancy and ruin
his reputation. Max must decide whether to turn
his back on the woman carrying his child or risk
everything, including his heart....

**Don't miss the next installment of
the Park Avenue Scandals series—
Front Page Engagement
by Laura Wright—
coming in August 2008
from Silhouette Desire!**

Always Powerful, Passionate and Provocative.

COMING NEXT MONTH

**#1879 HIGH-SOCIETY SECRET PREGNANCY—
Maureen Child**
Park Avenue Scandals
With her shocking pregnancy about to be leaked to the press, she
has no choice but to marry the millionaire with whom she spent
one passionate night.

#1880 DANTE'S WEDDING DECEPTION—Day Leclaire
The Dante Legacy
He'd lied and said he was her loving husband. For this Dante
bachelor had to discover the truth behind the woman claiming to
have lost her memory.

#1881 BOUND BY THE KINCAID BABY—Emilie Rose
The Payback Affairs
A will and an orphaned infant had brought them together. Now
they had to decide if passion would tear them apart.

#1882 BILLIONAIRE'S FAVORITE FANTASY—Jan Colley
She'd unknowingly slept with her boss! And now the billionaire
businessman had no intention of letting her get away.

#1883 THE CEO TAKES A WIFE—Maxine Sullivan
With only twelve months to produce an heir it was imperative he
find the perfect bride...no matter what the consequences!

#1884 THE DESERT LORD'S BRIDE—Olivia Gates
Throne of Judar
The marriage had been arranged. And their attraction, unexpected.
But would the heir to the throne choose the crown over the woman
in his bed?